BAT
CAVE

THE CRITTER CHRONICLES, BOOK 2

Pre-release reviews

Scott Bischke tackles one of the most vexing problems for bat ecologists. He presents a captivating allegory on the challenges of studying wild populations through an exploration of White-nose Syndrome.

—*Dr. Marty Zaluski, Montana State Veterinarian*

BAT CAVE reinvigorates the time-honored tradition of teaching through parables. Beneath the light-hearted banter and storyline are lessons of the utmost importance. Highly recommended for all ages.

—*Chris Beatty, Founder and Editor Emeritus, Ecopress*

Scott Bischke does a fantastic job of integrating current events into his allegories, and readers of all ages will benefit from his books. In BAT CAVE, immigration is represented through the lens of local and migrating bats. The local bats declare ownership and refuse to share space and resources with those who arrive in large numbers and look different, bringing to light the injustice and cruelty of refusing those in need. Such storytelling can lead to great discussions in the classroom and beyond regarding immigration, colonization, and the judgements we make based on such minor details of humanity. THE CRITTER CHRONICLES engages readers to appreciate the intricate lives of the animals with whom we share the planet, while addressing the struggles of society and science from a perspective that is both approachable and enjoyable!

—*Kelsey Green, Writing and Leadership Professor,*
Montana State University

BAT CAVE made me realize there was so much about bats I didn't know. I appreciated the story's strong message about working together and extending genuine friendship. Granted, such effort engages us in things that we are not comfortable with, and THAT was powerful. BAT CAVE asks us to both question science and trust science. As humans, we have that capacity, but sometimes don't use it or don't use it wisely.

—*Nancy Jordheim, Assistant Superintendent (retired),*
Fargo ND Public Schools

BAT CAVE is an entertaining story that also educates and invites critical thinking about our responsibilities to each other and the role of science within a civil society.

—*Kathy Brewer, Environmental Engineer*

BAT CAVE is an enjoyable tale filled with delightful characters! Much like FISH TANK, this book would be a wonderful reading/discussion activity in the classroom. I think the book will be enjoyed by a wide range of ages.

—*Jody Ouradnik, Education Curriculum Content Designer*

This charming allegory combines Scott's research, writing ability, and passion for addressing environmental harms while delighting and educating both the kids and their grown-ups. The critters' persuasive personalities rival those in FISH TANK with noble (human) traits like fairness and loyalty.

—*Lori Byron, MD, Pediatrician, and*
Chair of Montana Health Professionals for a Healthy Climate

BAT CAVE is a fabulously engaging story, written in such a way as to both capture the reader's attention and lead them through some timely pandemic issues of great concern. White-nose Syndrome in bats is an epidemic of catastrophic proportions (as the title suggests) and it is great that this issue is getting this kind of attention. This book should be widely used in schools at all levels everywhere.

—Dr. Lois Alexander, Professor of Biological Sciences,
College of Southern Nevada

I had a great time reading BAT CAVE. I find the epidemic topic fascinating—I had no idea that the white-nose epidemic existed, let alone that it has killed millions of bats. .... I recommend BAT CAVE because it's adventureful, you learn a bunch of amazing facts about bats, and I like the plot of the story.

—Brent Jordheim, Lawyer, Denver Public School System .... &
Reese (in her own words, after reading aloud with Dad), age 8

BAT CAVE is a fun read with a powerful and important message. A creative new way for non-scientists to interact with essential science concepts!
—Dr. Janet Lindsley, Professor of Biochemistry

I liked BAT CAVE. Bischke does an excellent job of leading the reader onwards into the story and I and suspect most readers will regard it as a bit of a page-turner. The story ties both disease and immigration/migration together. I like that those two topics are conjoined, because it's a reality of our time (or any time, for that matter), that issues can't be examined separately but have to be looked at as a whole. Multiple causation is hard for most of us to wrap our brains around, but it's also truth and reality.

—Linda Ashkenas, Ecologist

BAT CAVE is an intriguing journey that explores our important relationships with the natural world and our own human nature.

— *Dr. Winifred Frick, Chief Scientist,*
Bat Conservation International

In a heartwarming tale filled with unexpected twists, Bischke takes readers on a journey to Baja with an eagle and a seagull and numerous bats! The critters in BAT CAVE are captivating and the plot keeps you turning the pages. Bischke skillfully weaves science into the narrative to detail the struggles faced by these wild creatures, explaining concepts from migration to infectious diseases. An important subplot concerns the epidemic of White-nose Syndrome—a disease that is wiping out bats across much of North America—and how humans are trying to save the bats. BAT CAVE presents science in an exciting and engaging way, making the story perfect for all ages.

— *Dr. Raina Plowright,*
Professor of Disease Ecology, Cornell University

BAT CAVE is an interesting and compelling story with a certain *je ne sais quoi.*

—*William Gibson, Professional Pilot*

BAT CAVE provides a unique opportunity for folks of all ages to learn about science and human nature via the journey and experiences of the critters in this tale. Similar to FISH TANK, BAT CAVE brings important themes to life—this time, related to disease—through the book's animal protagonists. Bischke's allegorical approach allows, even forces, us human readers to think a little bit harder about critical issues, which I appreciate and think others will, too. A thoughtful and entertaining read.

—*Dr. Miranda Margetts,*
Assistant Research Professor, Montana State University

BAT CAVE is flat out wonderful! A mind-expanding, modern-day fable for all ages that makes you think, wonder, and care.

—Tom Vandel, author of THE BROKEN WORLD,
2022 High Plains Book Awards finalist

BAT CAVE is a powerful and entertaining allegory full of opportunities for rich exploration and discussion. The book takes us on an engaging adventure filled with delightful characters: most new, others old friends from the book's predecessor in the series, FISH TANK. Bischke tells a compelling story with themes such as friendship across cultural divides, public health strategies, immigration, and polarization. Conflicts in the storyline provide many big and difficult conversations that we are called to be a part of. BAT CAVE gives us a safe and easily accessible space to start those conversations. For the classroom—indeed for us all— BAT CAVE is an excellent resource to explore challenging concepts and engage in critical thought.

— Joan Exley,
Community Literacy Coordinator, Province of British Columbia

Scott Bischke's BAT CAVE: A FABLE OF EPIDEMIC PROPORTIONS is a fast-flying read that tells the tale of two feathered friends' journey to Mexico for the winter. Volant the eagle and Gabby the seagull end up wintering on an island that is home to two large bat colonies. As they befriend the bats and learn about their lifestyles, Volant and Gabby become embroiled in the mystery of the humans who come to the island and take away some of their bat friends. An engaging story seen from a bird's—and bat's—eye view, BAT CAVE also informs the reader about the devastating disease, White-nose Syndrome, which has killed millions of bats.

— Eva Silverfine, author of EPHEMERAL WINGS

BAT CAVE

A Fable of Epidemic Proportions

THE CRITTER CHRONICLES, BOOK 2

by
Scott Bischke

with artwork by Katie Lindberg

*   A MountainWorks Press Book   *
Bozeman, MT

Other books by Scott Bischke

TRUMPELSTILTSKIN – A Fairy Tale (MountainWorks Press 2016)

FISH TANK – A Fable for our Times
Book 1 in The Critter Chronicles series (MountainWorks Press 2012)

GOOD CAMEL, GOOD LIFE – Finding Enlightenment One Drop of Sweat at a Time (MountainWorks Press 2010)

CROSSING DIVIDES – A Couples' Story of Cancer, Hope, and Hiking Montana's Continental Divide
(American Cancer Society 2002)

TWO WHEELS AROUND NEW ZEALAND – A Bicycle Journey on Friendly Roads (Pruett Pub. hardback 1992; Ecopress paperback 1996)

BAT CAVE —
A Fable of Epidemic Proportions

Copyright © 2023 by Scott Bischke

ISBN 978-0-9825947-7-3   LCCN 2023934030

Publisher—MountainWorks Press

An imprint of MountainWorks, Incorporated

BAT CAVE is available in paperback, or Kindle and other eBook formats. A book club and classroom discussion guide can be downloaded from the author's website (*www.scottbischke.com*). Find Scott and his much-loved books on Amazon, Goodreads, and Linked In, or at the website just noted.

For the Bats —

May We All Learn

to Appreciate Their Importance

And for the Dedicated Researchers

Who Study Them

Author's Notes

I FIND JOY in allegories. Allegories allow readers to explore familiar topics from a distinctly unfamiliar viewpoint. The challenges and foibles, the heroes and those less heroic, of a fictional world—one mostly made up of talking animals!—can be seen through a kinder, more thoughtful lens. Allegories allow ready comparison with the "real" world, but with more room to consider and ponder, and less demand for black and white interpretations.

Simply put, an allegorical world is a less daunting place than the real one.

We have much to worry about in this day and age. Climate change—the topic of FISH TANK: A FABLE FOR OUR TIMES, Book 1 in THE CRITTER CHRONICLES series—is an existential threat to humanity and the biosphere. FISH TANK depicts that threat through the struggles of a community of fish whose world is an aquarium, and who are struggling with rising temperatures in a culture of intertwining issues: politics and power, science and misinformation, and the interests of community versus self. The book, much like this one, explores the interplay of such critical societal factors, and how (and if!) society can emerge from a crisis.

BAT CAVE: A FABLE OF EPIDEMIC PROPORTIONS—Book 2 in THE CRITTER CHRONICLES series—starts where FISH TANK left off. Here we consider other issues and controversies we are all too aware of in 2023, including pandemic diseases, vaccination sentiments, and immigration policies. BAT CAVE tackles these issues and more, this time through the lens of multiple colonies of bats living in a cave, some bats local, some migrating through.

While the underlying topics of BAT CAVE, like those of FISH TANK, are difficult ones, the critters and situations that bring these stories to the reader are written to be fun yet enlightening, quirky and challenging. Of great importance is this: the best thing about an allegory is that while the author can create a fictional world, full of engaging characters and interesting plot twists, it is up to the reader to consider and interpret that fictional world in the way they themselves see it.

It's important, I think, to let you the reader know that much science is incorporated into BAT CAVE (as it was in FISH TANK), sometimes gently, sometimes more directly. I provide a look at some of that science, albeit briefly, in the book's *Afterword*.

Notable: A BAT CAVE discussion guide for classrooms and book clubs can be downloaded from *www.scottbischke.com* (see the BAT CAVE page).

With those items as background, it is my fervent hope that you enjoy BAT CAVE: A FABLE OF EPIDEMIC PROPORTIONS, and that the story gives you pause for thought.

Scott Bischke

Bozeman, Montana, USA

May 2023

Critters of the bat cave, and beyond

Gabby	Western gull
Jessie	Sea turtle
Spouts	Gray whale
Volant	Bald eagle

Long-term bat residents of the big island

Sully	Lead California leaf-nosed bat
Sonar	California leaf-nosed bat (security lead)
Starr	California leaf-nosed bat
Peevy	Lead Pallid bat
Pushy	Pallid bat (security lead)
Prickly	Pallid bat

Migratory bats passing through

Lepto	Lead Lesser long-nosed bat
Luna	Lesser long-nosed bat
Flow	Lead Mexican free-tailed bat
Swift	Mexican free-tailed bat

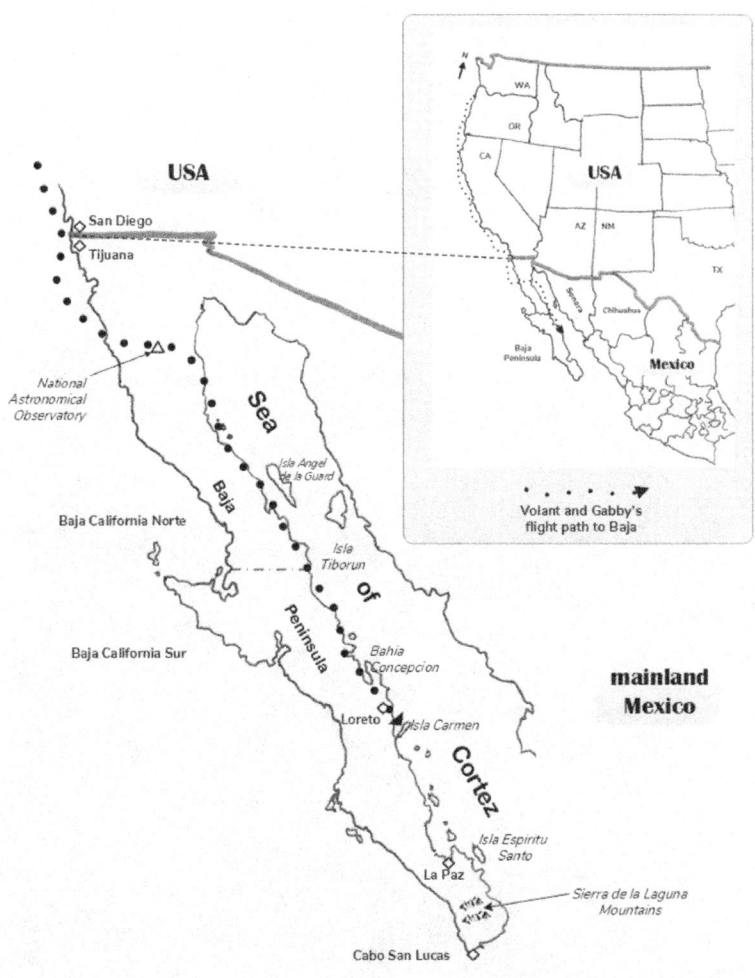

The flight to, and some geography of, the Baja Peninsula

For as the eyes of bats are to the blaze of day,
so is the reason in our soul to the things
which are by nature most evident of all.

— Aristotle

(Or, more simply, we people may not always
comprehend or accept truths that are
obvious or provable.)

Chapter 1

STREAKS OF CLOUDS colored the sky orange far out over the Pacific, leading to a golden sun glowing above the horizon. The Oregon Coast air carried a gentle breeze. The water along the shore stood strangely calm, barely a wave in sight.

High above Volant, a bald eagle, soared. She reveled in the peace and beauty of the late afternoon, wishing she could fly on deep into the night. But Mexico was still many days ahead, and Volant knew she needed to rest before continuing south.

With a sigh Volant turned her eyes downward, searching for a nighttime perch in one of the giant Douglas firs along the coast. Her gaze was suddenly interrupted, however, as a seagull, flying fast, cut directly under the eagle, barely two feet away.

As it passed the seagull flipped upside down and yelled up to Volant, "You think you're fast, do you old friend? Well Gabby caught you! And now I'm passing you, ya giant snail! I'm *The Fastest Flier in the Sky!*"

Before Volant could respond with how ridiculous that claim was and how she herself had just been lollygagging, Gabby the seagull flipped over and dive-bombed straight for the sea!

Volant gave a moment's thought to chasing down the cheeky gull, but then decided better of it. Instead, Volant shook her head and returned her attention to finding a landing spot on the forest edge. Soon she spotted a likely tree on a secluded inlet. She changed course for the tree, which she saw rose high above the lone house on the cove.

As Volant dropped toward her perch, a bent old man emerged from the house. The old man, who wore a tattered wool sweater, used a cane with one hand and carried a box in the other. He walked stiffly out toward the edge of the sea. The man's presence surprised Volant—the inlet wasn't a beach area where you'd expect to see people, but was instead a rough shoreline of craggy basalt and, most days, crashing waves.

At this moment, however, the sea stood silent. Volant dropped to the treetops, and then flared to land on a big dead limb lower down, just overhanging the house. Settling onto her perch, the eagle looked on with curiosity as the old man continued forward toward the edge of the ocean. Soon Volant realized she wasn't the only one watching—Gabby the seagull had reappeared, and was circling around the inlet, eyes intent on the happenings below.

Oblivious of his overseers, the old man walked on to the ocean's edge. Once there he set the box down at his feet, and then opened the lid. Quickly two crabs scrambled out the top of the box and raced across the basalt toward a large tide pool. The crabs paused briefly at the water's edge to team up and chase off a smaller crab. Then, as quickly as they had arrived at the tide pool, the crabs slipped under its inky water and disappeared.

"That's weird," thought Volant. "What is the old man doing with a couple of crabs?"

Volant had little time to ponder the question, as soon the old man looked up from watching the crabs and returned his attention to the box. He stooped down and carefully removed a turtle from the box.

"A turtle?" Volant thought, perplexed.

Ever so gingerly, the old man stepped to a lower level in the rock, so that he was now standing just a foot above the calm ocean waters. Volant watched as the old man turned the turtle toward himself, and then seemed to say something aloud.

In the next moment the old man leaned out over the water, and gently deposited the turtle in the sea.

As the old man walked back to the house, Volant turned her eyes to the ocean, to the place where the turtle bobbed silently. She saw the turtle turn its head back to the old man, a look of fear in its eyes.

And then another strange thing: The turtle appeared to shiver.

But before Volant had long enough to consider what the old man's strange behavior might mean, a white flash streaked down out of the sky. Abruptly Gabby the seagull splashed down next to the surprised turtle, showering it in spray.

Chapter 2

ARRIVING BACK AT his house, the Professor could not bear to go in, knowing what he would find. It was all gone, his dream destroyed.[1]

"Perhaps this is a sign," the Professor thought sadly. "I wonder if it's time for me to retire?"

The old man paused then, contemplating, knowing that making such a dramatic life change requires due diligence and deliberation. "Maybe I'm just being batty," he thought. "That's such a big question. Perhaps I'll ask my daughter when she returns from her travels."

Just then, a small fluttering movement high above caught the Professor's attention, pulling him out of his thoughts. He raised his eyes to a broken board in the roof eave. There, hiding in a dark recess, hung a small bat.

While bats had found their way into his aquarium cave a time or two over the years, he'd never seen one under the roof of the house, plus this one seemed somehow different. It wasn't so much

---

[1] Or was it? You can find out by reading TURTLE RETREAT: A FABLE OF DEADLY CONSEQUENCES, a follow-on book in THE CRITTER CHRONICLES series!

the mousey ears that caught his eye, but instead the mottled-looking nose—wait, was it white? Hmm, tough to tell in the shadows.

The Professor gave his head an inquisitive tilt, still looking at the bat, then said, "What is that on your nose?" The bat, for its part, huddled deeper into the recess, its nose now hidden.

The Professor paused, considering this new question. He drew in a long, grimacing breath, wondering if he should be concerned. As he opened the door to enter the house, the Professor thought of exactly who he could ask to shed some light on the mystery of the mottled nose.

Chapter 3

WHILE THE PROFESSOR was considering the bat, and then stepping into his house, Gabby the seagull was busy trying to help the shivering turtle.

"Be careful" yelled the turtle, after Gabby splashed into the ocean next to her. "Didn't you s-s-see me?"

"Of course I saw you," Gabby returned. "That's why I'm here! You looked so miserable while I was flying over I decided to drop in and find out what's wrong. What's your name anyway, and why do you look so sad?"

"J-J-Jessie," stammered the sea turtle, "my name is Jessie. I used to live in a fish tank under the Professor's house up there."

"What in heaven's name are you talking about?" said Gabby the seagull, confused. "A fish tank? Where? What? Why? How? ... I don't understand."

Jessie shivered through a long and winding story about all that had happened to the Professor's underground aquarium.[2] The turtle's quavering

---

[2] If you don't know the story, find out what happened by reading FISH TANK: A FABLE FOR OUR TIMES, Book 1 in THE CRITTER CHRONICLES series!

voice lifted somewhat at the start of the story, then grew increasingly sad and downhearted as she progressed. When Jessie closed her story with, "...and that's how I ended up here," Gabby let out a long sigh of empathy.

"Goodness, gracious," said Gabby, pausing for a moment to contemplate Jessie's story. "I am so sorry for all you have faced. I take it that was the Professor I saw drop you in the sea?"

"Y-y-yes, that was him," returned Jessie.

"But why? What was he thinking?" Gabby said. "You are clearly not from here, look how you shiver in these cold Oregon waters."

"The P-p-professor was so distraught about all that had happened, I don't think he *was* thinking," said Jessie. "And you're r-r-right, I'm from farther south, where the w-w-water is warmer. But I was c-c-captured as a hatchling, then passed from hand to hand until s-s-someone gave me to the Professor and he t-t-took care of me..."

"...until everything changed," said Gabby, finishing Jessie's thought.

"Yes," said Jessie. "He was s-s-so upset I don't think what clearly should have registered—that I wasn't meant to l-l-live in the ocean here—dawned on him."

"Indeed," said Gabby, before pausing in thought. "Look," Gabby finally said, "why don't you climb out on that rock shelf over there while I see if I can figure something out. It'll be warmer for you."

And with that the seagull flapped its wings, and flew off.

Chapter 4

VOLANT THE EAGLE had grown curious watching the seagull and turtle talk. So much so that the eagle thought to seek out Gabby the seagull and find out what they'd spoken about. But that didn't turn out to be necessary for as soon as Gabby got airborne, the seagull pointed straight for Volant.

Gabby quickly circled in and landed on the crest of the house, just below the big limb where Volant was perched.

"That turtle, Jessie, needs some help," said Gabby before Volant could say a thing.

"I don't wonder," said the eagle. "It surely doesn't belong here. I often see turtles like—who did you say, Jessie?—yes like Jessie far down the coast during those winters I head south. Did she say what she's doing here?"

"It was a confusing story," returned Gabby, "filled with an underground aquarium and rising temperatures and crabs and an old professor. I don't think I could explain it well, but suffice it to say for now Jessie is on her own and out of her element. Poor thing is freezing."

"Yes," said Volant, "I could see her shivering from here."

"*Of course* you could see that from all the way up here," said Gabby with a bit of envy, "with those *eagle* eyes of yours. But the question is what can we do to help? That's why I flew up here, hoping you might have some idea."

Volant tilted her head to the side, silent and thinking. "We need to get Jessie to warmer waters, like down in Mexico. I am going that way myself, I've decided. I thought I'd stick out the winter here again but this is the first day of the New Year, and I've been chilled to the bone for a month. So Mexico it will be for the rest of the winter. Not that I could carry Jessie that far, so that's no help... Hmmm, what to do, what to do...."

Volant fell silent, looking down at Jessie who by now had climbed onto shore. A long silence followed. Then the eagle lifted her gaze from Jessie far out to sea; a moment later Gabby swore Volant's golden eyes began to shine in the last glow of the sunset.

"I think I have an idea," said Volant triumphantly. "We can make it happen in the morning."

Chapter 5

EARLY THE NEXT morning, Volant the eagle and Gabby the seagull met again. "Ah, good," said Volant, looking out to the ocean. "He's still here."

Gabby followed Volant's eyes out over the water just in time to see a giant puff of mist blast into the air. "Hold it, what?" Gabby exclaimed. "Spouts? You're thinking that old gray whale can help?"

"Why not?" Volant replied. "Spouts is headed south now, down to the warmer waters where Jessie needs to be."

"But Spouts is kind of a wet blanket. I doubt he'll…"

"So what?" interrupted the eagle, undeterred. "Spouts owes us."

"He does?"

"You help Spouts find krill sometimes don't you?" Volant asked.

"True," replied Gabby, more than a bit of pride now in his voice. "I have a better view from the air, plus I can fly a lot faster when I'm looking than Spouts can swim." Gabby paused with a mischievous look in his eye, then continued, "I *am*, after all, *The Fastest Flier in the* ..."

"Do *not* start with me again," Volant glared down, "or I will jump down there and put you in your web-footed place!"

"Sorry, just having a bit of feathered fun," said Gabby, still playful. "I mean let's face it, I am just one letter shy of being an *eagull* myself!"

That broke the mood, drawing a raised eyebrow and a short chuckle from Volant. The eagle released Gabby from her piercing look, turning her eyes back to the sea just in time to see Spouts lifting his big tail out of the water to dive.

After the whale disappeared, Volant returned to the topic at hand, looking back to Gabby and saying, "And let's not forget that I once warned Spouts about the pod of killer whales coming his way."

"Ah, yes, I had forgotten about that," said the seagull. This time Gabby turned to look out to sea and without turning back to the eagle said, "He *does* sort of owe us, doesn't he?"

"Indeed he does. Look, Spouts will be back to the surface in a few minutes," said Volant. "Why don't you fly out there and wait? When Spouts comes up, ask if Jessie can ride south with him. I'd go myself but Spouts might take a bit of convincing and I'm not quite as well designed for landing on water as you."

At the subtle compliment from the grand eagle Gabby's chest puffed out more than a little.

"Will you quit all your silly primping?!" Volant growled, though with a smile in her tone. "I'm still ten times faster than you! Now just go!"

And with that the eagle jumped down to the roof edge where the seagull perched, then flipped her big wing to knock Gabby off into the air.

Volant watched while Gabby winged out to sea, hung on the breeze for a time, then settled onto the water to wait for Spouts to surface again. When the big whale at last blew topside a hundred meters away, Volant saw the seagull lift off the water and head that way. Volant could see Gabby hover above the whale for a moment, then drop down and land right on Spouts' back.

Chapter 6

VOLANT THE EAGLE looked below to see Jessie the turtle, alternately shivering and trying to climb upward toward the house. The turtle was having no luck whatsoever, stymied at every turn by insurmountable rocks or the rugged basalt ridges.

Taking pity, Volant swooped down and landed next to the exasperated turtle.

"What are you doing?" Volant said.

"I must get back to the house and find my friends!" Jessie exclaimed, trying to climb over a rocky step but becoming unbalanced and tipping back.

"Your friends? In the house? What?" asked Volant, confused.

"Yes, Tommy and Doc and Altair and Ally and Gabe and Zuriela and Dusty and…." Jessie's voice tailed away in sadness as she tried climb once again.

"Hold it a minute," Volant said. "Just take a breath, my friend. It's Jessie, right? That's what my seagull friend told me. You'll never make it up there, I'm sorry about that; and I'm sorry for whatever might have happened to your friends. Can you tell me about it?"

AN HOUR LATER, waves had begun to break against the shore as Jessie the turtle completed her story. "So that's what I know," concluded Jessie.

Volant sighed in sympathy. "I am so very sorry," Volant said. "Your aquarium compatriots sound like they were a good group."

"Mostly, yes, m-m-mostly they were ... I mean they *are*," Jessie murmured in agreement. Eyes downcast in despair, Jessie fell silent and still. Suddenly a cold wave broke over the rocky shore showering Jessie and causing Volant to jump back. In another moment, a big shiver shook the turtle's body.

"You are cold, my new friend," Volant said, at once protective but also happy for a change of topic. "I can see you shivering even from up in the tree, and last night must have been miserable. I daresay you do not belong in these cold waters. I've never seen anyone like you here before. To the south, where I

fly many winters, yes I've seen your kind. But here?
No, not here, at least not that I recall."

"I d-d-don't know," Jessie stammered. "I was so
small when I was t-t-taken from my home. But I do
know you are right about one thing: I am very, v-v-
very cold."

Chapter 7

VOLANT THE EAGLE and Gabby the seagull were once again perched on the roof crest of the Professor's home, both looking out to sea.

"So very good of Spouts," Volant was saying. "I knew that grumpy old whale had a soft heart."

"Wasn't even that hard," Gabby replied. "Said he'd be happy for the company given that it's such a long haul to warmer waters."

"Indeed," said Volant, her thoughts turning to starting the long flight to Mexico the next day.

"Hey, can you see Jessie?" Gabby asked, pulling Volant out of her thoughts. "I can see Spouts but can't make out Jessie…"

"Yes, I see our new turtle friend quite clearly," said Volant. "Jessie is hanging onto Spouts' back and…"

"…and there they go!" shouted Gabby, interrupting as Spouts' tail lifted high into the air. "Safe voyage you two!"

"Yes, safe voyage," agreed Volant, eyes suddenly brightening. "But hey, perhaps not just two! Take a closer look my friend. Just past that last big wave are more spouts, white-sided dolphins by the looks of it, chasing after them!"

Chapter 8

THE NEXT MORNING Gabby the seagull, flying up the coast, spotted Volant the eagle sitting in her tree perch above the Professor's roof. Behind Volant the sun peaked its head over the Coast Range; in front of her the breaking waves pounded the inlet's rocky shoreline.

Gabby bee-lined for the tree, banked hard, bounced off a limb, then came to a crashing halt besides Volant.

"*Fastest Flier in the Sky*, or so I hear," quipped Volant, grabbing Gabby before he fell out of the tree. "But with the *worst* landing gear ever!"

"Fair point, my friend," said Gabby, finally finding a spot on the perch flat enough to stand. "Maybe my gear isn't any better suited for landing in treetops than yours is for landing on the sea."

"Touché," responded Volant. "We all have our special talents, don't we?"

"Yes, we do … to do … uh … what we do… Oh never mind!" said a tongue-twisted Gabby.

Volant chuckled.

"And speaking of doing," Gabby continued, looking up at the eagle, "do you really need to leave today? Feels like you only just arrived. Why don't you just stay in Oregon? A few years back you over-wintered here."

"Yes, and a miserable wet winter it was as I recall, just like the last month!" Volant looked out on the ocean, where at the moment a fog bank was rising near at hand; behind that ominous dark clouds approached.

"No," Volant continued, "I think I'll try my luck south again for the rest of this winter. I like the warmth, plus I like seeing new country. I've been to New Mexico, southern California, even to the Mexican mainland coast, but this time I'm thinking to have a look at the Baja Peninsula."

"Baja?" said Gabby.

"Yes, Baja. Hey, listen," Volant said, her voice taking on a new tone, "why don't you come with me?"

"Me? Seriously?" returned Gabby.

"Sure," said Volant. "Lots of your western gull friends head to Baja. Why not you? You always say you want to travel, get away for the winter, but then never do. Here's your chance."

Gabby looked skeptical, responding, "Oh, I don't know if...."

"Afraid you won't be able to keep up," needled Volant, interrupting. "I thought you were *The Fastest Flier in the Sky*?!"

"Really," said Gabby. "That's how you're going to play this?"

"Yep, slowpoke, that's how I'm going to play it." And without another word, Volant the eagle launched into the air, pointed south, with not so much as a glance back.

Twenty minutes on, as Volant crossed over a headland far down the coast, a white streak flashed past the eagle, an inch away, throwing the big bird into a momentary spin.

Volant righted herself with a smile, ready for the inevitable as the seagull raced back to taunt her.

"So you think you're fast?" Gabby challenged. "I'm going to leave you in the dust from here all the way to Baja! And then back! Better get used to it, you banana slug, I'm *The Fastest Flier in the Sky!*"

Chapter 9

THE FLIGHT SOUTH, especially during the first week, turned out to be far tougher on Gabby the seagull than Volant the eagle. Not long into day three, Gabby's cries of, "*The Fastest Flier in the Sky!*" even fell silent, replaced by periodic groans and squawks.

It wasn't that Gabby wasn't capable—he'd once flown to the Alvord Desert from the coast in two days, averaging almost 200 miles a day! Still, by the middle of day five the battered seagull had taken to flying in the big eagle's draft, finding the going much easier.

Near sunset on day seven, the two friends soared high over a great bay along the ocean. Below them to the south, on both sides of the bay, stretched an endless city of houses and buildings and roads. But Gabby was far more interested in the orange bridge right underneath them.

"Let's call it a day," said Gabby, coming up alongside Volant.

Volant followed Gabby's gaze to the bridge. "On the bridge tower? Hmm, lots of cars, could be noisy. And what about the wind?"

"I don't care my friend. I'm tired and my shoulders are sore." Without another word the seagull pointed down and was gone, moments later making an awkward landing atop one of the orange bridge towers.

Volant the eagle circled the tower more thoughtfully, then landed more gracefully, with a big flap of the wings at the last moment to slow herself.

Settled, the eagle picked up the conversation where they'd left it a thousand feet higher in the air. "Sore shoulders," said Volant. "Really? Even with all the drafting you're doing? And hold it, what about the time you flew 200 miles inland in a day? Heck, we're only doing half of that each day!"

"Two hundred, two *shmundred*," Gabby returned. "That was a fluke. I hate flying away from the ocean, but I had the west wind behind me the entire flight so decided to see how far I could go. Why haven't you ever asked me how long it took to fly *back* to the coast?"

Before Volant could answer a sudden wind gust blasted the tower, almost knocking both birds into the air. "OK, this isn't going to work," Volant said. "Let's get to somewhere lower or we're not going to get any sleep tonight. Tomorrow's another full day of flying."

When Gabby nodded reluctant agreement, Volant dove off the tower into the fading light. Gabby followed, noting that Volant was at first pointed toward an island far out in the middle of the bay, but then thought better of it and swerved ninety degrees right, straight toward the city.

Gabby followed dutifully, wondering where Volant was headed, until far below, silhouetted against the darkening sky, he saw a small group of redwood trees jutting up above the streets.

Dropping lower and lower, Gabby started to feel small bumps against his wings, first a few, then a volley, then non-stop. The seagull suddenly realized that in failing light he had unwittingly flown into a vast swarm of bugs! In the next moment, a miniature missile rocketed by—so like a small bird but then again not—then another raced past, then another and another, each twisting and turning and flitting and flying and darting and here one second and gone the next!

What on Earth?

By the time Gabby reached the crown of the redwoods, Volant had already landed, thankfully on such a big flat top that even the tired seagull could manage a respectable landing in the near darkness.

"Did you see that?" asked Gabby.

"The million bugs, you mean?" replied Volant.

"No…well yes…but no I mean those flying menaces racing back and forth through the bug swarm!"

"Oh those," said Volant, unperturbed. "You mean the bats. A whole lot more here than we see on the Oregon coast, that's for sure. Speedy little guys, aren't they?"

Chapter 10

VOLANT THE EAGLE and Gabby the seagull woke at dawn. Cold, dense fog, rolling into the bay from the ocean, covered most of the orange bridge. Only the tower where the two friends had landed the evening before rose out of the clouds.

Far below Volant and Gabby, a sleepy city showed the first signs of waking. Less sleepy—and nearer at hand—were the still fluttering bats, dive-bombing back and forth across the sky.

By the time the sun glowed just below the horizon, the bat swarm had moved closer to the redwoods. Some of the bats yelled among themselves, others remained silent, dutifully snapping up the last of the bugs still flying about. Sometimes it seemed as if the bats might smash into the two birds, only to veer off just before impact. Several times Gabby yelled, "Hey! Watch it you little gremlins!"

"They're fine, calm down, they're good fliers," said Volant, "and fast, too!"

"Not that fast," Gabby said sourly. "I could show them a thing or two!"

"Oh calm down, you silly bird," Volant chuckled. "They're just ruffling your feathers a bit. We could take off and get out of here if we wanted. But I think a longer rest would do us good."

Gabby, tired as he was, nodded in agreement, though followed with a muttered, "Harrumph!"

So the birds sat and watched the bats fly as the sun slowly cleared the horizon. Along the way, they noticed that one-by-one the bats began to settle, landing under the canopy of the redwoods just below them.

"Thank goodness," said Gabby after all the bats had landed. Then the seagull crept to the edge of the perch where he and Volant rested, and leaned far out and over, ducking and twisting his head to peer below the branches and almost tumbling into space. Straightening back up, Gabby exclaimed, "Talk about a head rush—the bats are all perched upside down!"

Hours later, well into morning, Volant sensed a movement and came awake, shaking her head to clear the cobwebs. Flitting haphazardly by was a lone bat, weak and unsteady in its flight. "Strange," thought the big bird, "all the other bats have been in their roost for hours, why is this one still out flying in the middle of the morning? And why is it so shaky?"

After the bat departed, Volant looked over at the still-sleeping seagull. The big eagle stretched her wings far and wide, paused to enjoy the feel of a light wind for a moment, then nudged Gabby awake.

"Time we be going," Volant said. "We've had a few extra hours off, days are short, and Baja isn't getting any closer."

Gabby yawned a great yawn, before doing his own little seagull shudder. Looking at Volant, he spoke in a strong voice, "That extra sleep really helped. Now I'm ready to go, raring to go actually, to show you my tailfeath…"

Suddenly the lone bat returned, careening right and left and buzzing right over Gabby, parting his head feathers as if a comb had been run through them. Gabby never saw it, just felt the whoosh.

"What was that!?" Gabby shouted.

"One of the bats," Volant returned.

"A bat, now, in daylight?" asked Gabby.

"Indeed, I saw it a few moments ago, as well. Out in daylight and really wobbly—very strange behavior for a bat," said Volant, head tilting, eyes narrowed. "I wonder what that's all about."

Chapter 11

REJUVENATED FROM THE half-day rest, and floating on friendly winds, the two travelers made rapid progress south. Gabby the seagull no longer complained about sore shoulders and even flew in front so Volant the eagle could draft him from time to time. Only once did the friends detour from the coastline, heading out to sea to hopscotch down a group of islands. They sought to avoid the hustle and bustle of the largest mass of humanity either bird had ever seen, including an endless stream of jets coming and going.

On day 14 after starting south—and now back following the coastline—Volant and Gabby began to see a smaller city unfold before them. In time, they crossed high above a massive bay reaching inland from the ocean, and Volant nodded to an interesting assortment of red roofs. They pushed on and the city slowly faded, until they passed a river and the country became more open, with few structures.

Volant signaled to Gabby that it was time for a rest and pointed herself downward. As the two birds dropped, they saw an odd-looking fence stretching inland from the coast as far as even Volant's eyes could make out. *Odd looking*, that is, because the fence was so tall, plus at the beach the fence ran straight out into the waves before finally being swallowed by the sea.

Beyond the fence to the south the emptiness abruptly ended. Another city pushed itself against the boundary as if by sheer force it could bow the fence and eventually break it.

Volant and Gabby circled in along the beach looking for a place to land. Eventually Gabby dropped to the sand where other seagulls had gathered, while Volant landed high atop the strange fence.

Volant settled in to rest, first checking on Gabby, then looking more closely at the big fence she had perched atop. The big eagle noticed that the fence, made up of rugged metal posts and slats, was as thick and solid as it was high. The fence—more of a wall, actually—appeared impossible to cross unless you could fly over it, or tunnel under it, or were the size of a mouse and could pass through the small gaps in the slats.

As Volant studied the barrier, two people, talking excitedly, approached the fence below her. It was an old woman and a younger man. Both were pointing north through slats in the wall, now yelling. When Volant lifted her head she saw two people running toward the wall from the other side, a younger woman with a small girl, perhaps four or five.

The four of them—the older woman and young man on one side, the young woman with the small girl pressed in front of her on the other side—met at the wall just below Volant, oblivious to the eagle perched above. The excited shouts turned to tears; everyone but the small girl alternatively sobbed and gently muttered proclamations of love.

The young woman pushed up against the wall, the young girl squeezed in front of her, the young man and old woman doing the same. It was as if they were willing the wall to come down so that they might hold each other, touch each other. It would not be, as they knew, and in a moment the young woman spread her hands apart and pushed her fingers through the fence slats. The young man held one of the young woman's hands as best he could; the old woman grabbed her other hand.

They stood like that for a time, the young man and young woman looking into each other's eyes. And then the young man pressed his lips into a gap in the slats, barely meeting the young woman's lips. For a moment, the ocean waves quieted and time stood still.

When the couple released their kiss, big smiles followed. They wiped the tears and excitement returned to their voices. The young man bent to greet the small girl, as the older woman looked over his shoulder. The small girl, so suddenly the group's focus, wrapped her arms around the young woman's legs, but never once did she stop looking at the young man.

And in that moment tears returned, first from the older woman, and then from the couple.

When they looked up a man in uniform had arrived. "I'm sorry," he said, "your three minutes are up." When no one moved, the man in uniform said more abruptly, "El tiempo terminado. No más, por favor. Vámonos."

Reluctantly the four people backed away from the fence, the young man shouting to the young woman and cupping his hand to his ear as if holding a phone. The young woman shook her head yes, then turned to walk back up the coast, holding the small girl's hand, the uniformed man close behind.

When the young woman looked back over her shoulder one last time, the small girl broke away, sprinting out onto the beach. The young woman raced out and caught the small girl, but not before she had scattered a flock of seagulls into the sky.

Chapter 12

THE TWO FRIENDS continued flying down the coast another day and a half until Volant the eagle suddenly turned inland, bidding Gabby the seagull to follow. Though Gabby had spent plenty of time inland, he hesitated, hovering, as leaving the ocean always gave him a queasy stomach. Still, when Volant circled back and assured him that they'd soon enough find salt water again, Gabby reluctantly followed.

The two friends climbed up over foothills until they were flying over rugged mountains. The Pacific Ocean had fallen away and was now just a shimmer on the horizon behind them.

Deep cuts and green pine forest soon dominated the landscape below. The sun had dipped toward the horizon and Gabby signaled it might be time to settle in for the night. Searching, Volant spotted a white dome sitting on the highest mountaintop around. Volant nodded to the strange sight and Gabby shrugged his shoulders. Having little else to guide them, the birds plunged earthward, ready to call it a day.

As they circled down to the big white dome, Volant and Gabby saw a car far back down the valley winding its way upward, popping in and out of view as it passed through the forest. Looking back below them, the two friends saw that the big white dome sat atop a circular, three-story building at the end of the road. It was so large the top was almost flat, making for an easy landing.

No one seemed about. Volant and Gabby settled in and watched night arrive. The last rays of a cold sun held to the mountaintop as shadows climbed up toward them. The line separating day from night moved up the three-story building, then up the curve of the dome. Soon the line crossed over them, a cool breeze accompanying its movement, and the two friends found themselves immersed in the darkness of twilight. Above, thousands of stars soon began to twinkle in the sky.

"Cool," said Gabby.

"Cool, indeed," said Volant with a bit of a shiver. "And tonight will be a *cool* one—almost feels like snow, doesn't it? Not to worry! Let's get some sleep and then tomorrow we'll get back to the coast— albeit a different coast—and point south again. It shouldn't take us too many more days to find warmer temperatures!"

SLEEP, IT TURNS out, did not come easily to the two birds that night. Barely had they drifted off when a car came chugging around the corner and into the parking lot below, alongside the three-story building. Shortly, with the engine killed and headlights extinguished, two people emerged, speaking enthusiastically as they began to unload gear in the dark.

Volant and Gabby exchanged a glance, with a silent "What is going on?" look passing between them.

Soon, one of the people opened a door into the building. A light splashed out on the ground in a skewed rectangle that reached to the car. The two people made several trips to move gear inside, and then the door shut and all went dark again.

Quiet returned and the eagle and the seagull began to drift back to sleep. But again, it was not to be. Suddenly the birds heard a great cranking noise and the domed roof began to move right under them! The roof groaned as it rolled back causing the birds to jump in fright. Light shot out of the growing gap between the building wall and the receding roof and then something else: bats!

A dozen bats shot out of the gap, almost smashing into Volant and Gabby. The birds had only time to jump away, though Gabby thought he noticed something funny as one of the bats passed by:

the bat had a small projection growing straight up and out of its nose.

Gabby had no time to consider the oddity. In another moment, the roof had receded enough that the two birds were in danger of their feet getting pinched under the stationary part of the roof.

"We gotta go!" screamed Volant. "Jump, Gabby, jump now!" The birds hopped into flight just as the last bit of roof where they could stand disappeared.

The two friends found a nearby rocky crag and made a shaky landing by the light spewing out of the dome. Looking back, they saw the lights from the dome suddenly blink out, the roof still open, and a dark sky filled with sparkling stars regained the night.

Chapter 13

BY NOON THE next day, peculiarities of the previous night set aside, the two friends could see a new coastline ahead, and another sea, just as Volant had promised. Below and farther north the sea flattened into the land. They could see a channel running through the flats, but it seemed to hold water only intermittently, which felt unnatural. And what looked like it should be muddy flats, instead appeared mostly cracked, dry, and shimmering in the sun.

Upon reaching the sea, Volant the eagle and Gabby the seagull turned away from the strange delta, pointing now down the coast. A strong wind rocketed them southward and Gabby did a little airborne jig of the wings.

"Well *you* sure seem less grumpy than last night," Volant joked.

"It's the sea," said Gabby, grinning. "Just knowing the water is there makes me feel more at ease."

"I'm that way, too," said Volant, "but it's thermals and tailwinds that make me happy."

"I like those, too!" said Gabby. Then, rolling sideways, Gabby flicked his wing in salute and shot off on the breeze, voice trailing behind, *"Fastest Flier in the Sky!"*

That gave Volant a smile, and she took off in a tear to catch her cheeky companion.

Chapter 14

THE TWO FRIENDS pushed along the coast for several days, enjoying the ever-increasing warmth. To their right Volant and Gabby looked down on a rugged dryland peninsula; to their left crystal blue waters. The coastline formed the glue that held the two together, and they clung to it as their guide.

One day Volant the eagle and Gabby the seagull passed between a long island and the peninsula. They talked of staying there for the winter, and even pulled up to sleep. But the cool night convinced them to continue south in the morning.

On dozens of occasions in the following days Volant and Gabby saw the big puffs of mist out in the sea as whales broke the surface, sometimes alone, sometimes in pods. One of the birds—usually Gabby—always dropped down to see if it might be Spouts the whale and Jessie the turtle, from back in Oregon. But no luck; only once was it a gray whale and that one wasn't Spouts.

At one point, the two friends passed over an enormous, rectangular bay reaching inland, then crossed over dry, barren country before coming back to the sea. Both were weary from the days of long-distance flying, and Gabby flew up alongside Volant to say so.

"Probably warm enough last night," said Gabby. "I think it's time we stop for the winter."

"Yes, must say I'm feeling it, too," replied Volant.

"We could go back to that big bay we just passed," said Gabby hopefully. "That looked good to me. What do you say?"

Volant tilted her head, as if unsure. "Maybe," she said, "but don't turn around yet. Look down the coast—see that beautiful island, and then behind it another one, even larger? And over on the peninsula there's a nice looking town. Lots to explore. I say we head for that big island."

"I've been exploring for weeks, my friend, and I am worn…"

Volant interrupted Gabby before he finished the thought, "…*plus* it's just a bit further south and so just a bit warmer. Come on, what do you say?"

And with that, Volant rocketed off, newly energized. Gabby shook his head, then pushed on in pursuit of his eagle friend.

SUNSET WAS UPON them as the two birds dropped to the island Volant had declared their winter home. They settled on top a lone palapa they found there. Behind them, the island's center grew up dry and tall, rugged and majestic. The palapa sat on a vacant beach that curved into the distance around a beautiful bay before ending at a craggy headland. The rock outcrop there rose vertically straight out of the sea.

A gentle breeze—so gentle it scarcely rustled the fronds of the palapa—came off the water below them, carrying the scent of the sea. The air remained warm and comfortable. Slowly the sun dropped to the horizon. Soon only three quarters of the sun remained visible, then just a half. Thin clouds streaked the sky—first in pink, then peach, then increasingly blood orange. As the sun blinked out below the horizon to the west, purple became the color of the sky to the east.

Through it all the two friends remained silent, watching. Stars appeared in the blackening sky, first by ones and twos, then by the hundreds, then by the thousands. Below them a sea lion, its head barely visible, swam along the shore's edge before turning out to open water. A thousand twinkling lights, almost as if a mirror of the sky, traced the sea lion's path through the sea.

Watching it all unfold, Gabby finally let out a sigh and said quietly, almost reverently, "OK, you're right, my friend. I think this will do us for the rest of the winter just fine."

Chapter 15

THE FOLLOWING MORNING Volant the eagle and Gabby the seagull explored the island, looking for a place to call their winter home. They settled on the high promontory they'd seen the night before, the one at the end of the beach where the palapa sat. A rocky pinnacle topped the promontory. Just below that was a flat ledge backed by a single, giant cactus. The cactus partially hid the rocky peak behind. The promontory was open on three sides: one side looked out over the sea; the second side looked down at the beach; the third side looked out to the distant town on the peninsula.

Visitors arrived that day. Some—for example cormorants, pelicans, boobies, and gulls—were expected. Likewise, Volant and Gabby were not surprised to see a couple of boats speed toward their island from the town on the peninsula. The first boat arrived about midday, pulling up to the palapa where the birds had spent the previous night. A half-dozen people in swimsuits jumped out to splash in the ocean and play on the beach. Much food was on display and Gabby vowed to check if any had been left behind once the people departed.

The second boat—far older and scarred—arrived late afternoon, after the first boat had departed. This boat had four people and, unlike the first group, these people seemed filled with purpose. They came ashore, but then rather than swimwear they put on white suits, gloves, and masks. Three of them carried equipment of some sort and the fourth carried a backpack and a big camera. They appeared to be exploring the island and once disappeared from view below the promontory for 90 minutes. When the group reemerged, their hunched shoulders signaled disappointment. They stripped off their whites suits, without energy, then climbed back into the boat, pushed off, and sped away back to the peninsula.

Later, yet another set of visitors arrived, and this group did catch Volant and Gabby totally off guard. The two birds had settled in for the first night at their new home, the rocky promontory. As with the previous sunset, they expected to watch the night peacefully unfold. But as the sun touched the horizon the quiet around Volant and Gabby was suddenly interrupted by a chirp behind them, then ten chirps, then hundreds—a full, crushing, discordant symphony of chirps!

"What is happening?" Gabby exclaimed.

Volant started to shrug her shoulders when suddenly a mini-missile whizzed overhead, and then another, and then another and another. Looking back, the birds could see the speeding projectiles bursting out from behind the big cactus. Peering closer, the birds realized the little rockets were coming out of a cut in the rock face behind the cactus, apparently a narrow cave entrance.

"Bat visitors," said Volant, unperturbed.

The chirping sound became overwhelming, as a hundred bats turned into a thousand bats emerging from the cave, massing and swirling together as if a small tornado. Volant remained quiet through it all while Gabby ducked and bobbed incessantly. For their part, the bats simply split around the birds as if they were boulders in a stream.

When the bat swarm emerging from the cave finally subsided, Gabby yelled at Volant, "*Visitors*?! What do you mean, *visitors*?! How about *pests*!"

"Or better yet…" It was a new voice, sharp and strong. "…how about *neither* of those?!"

Both Volant and Gabby pulled up short. They turned to find that one of the bats had landed in the pitted wall behind them, just to the side of the big cactus. The bat was addressing them from an upside down perch, its feet grasped to the rock.

"The only *visitors* and *pests* here...," growled a second voice, causing Gabby and Volant to lift their eyes higher to see another perched bat.

"...are you two!" Came a third, even more heated voice, this time another bat just to the right of the second one.

"Excuse me?" said Gabby, eyes spinning and clearly flummoxed.

"We bats have lived in this cave forever, we belong here!" shrieked yet another voice, this bat lower and to the left of the first.

"So it's you two," sneered a fifth bat, "who are the *visitors!*"

"And, I dare say, it's you two who are also the *pests*." Volant's gaze returned to the original speaker, the group's apparent leader, who continued matter-of-factly, "Because you two are standing right in our flight pattern."

Chapter 16

EVEN IN THE dim light it quickly became apparent to Volant the eagle and Gabby the seagull that they were facing a council of six bats. Equally apparent, and similarly unexpected, was that several of the bats had a curious leaf-like protrusion for a nose, while several others were somewhat pale in color.

Though the birds were far larger than the bats, Gabby still gave an involuntary shudder. Volant, on the other hand, looked at the bats calmly, then said, "First, my new friends, our apologies—until a few minutes ago we had no idea there was a cave behind the big cactus, much less a bat colony."

"Colon*ies*," said the bat leader coolly.

"Pardon me, *colonies*," Volant repeated. "Look, there's plenty of room. We can all share this space. Gabby and I can simply move aside or fly to a different perch when you all come and go—pretty much dusk and dawn, right? Sound good?"

The bats looked skeptical, but before any of them could respond negatively Volant continued, "Such decisions are just logistics we can figure out. Better we start with introductions. I am Volant and my seagull friend here is Gabby. We spent the last couple of weeks flying down the coast from the north, all the way from Oregon. Now…"

"*Fastest Flier in the Sky*," Gabby muttered under his breath.

"Forgive my friend," Volant continued, rolling her eyes as if sharing a silent—"See what I put up with?"—thought with the bats. "Now who are all of you?"

The bat leader, the one with the biggest nose, said, "My name is Sully. I'm the leader of the Leaf-nosed bats." Sully's voice remained solid and unwavering, but Volant noted the bat had softened its tone from earlier. "Over there above me," Sully said, nodding his head, "are Sonar and Starr, both from our colony."

Sonar stayed silent, but nodded coolly. Starr, who had yet to say anything and who Volant noticed had shimmering eyes, said dreamily, "Hola."

"And you three," Volant said addressing the three pale bats before Gabby could start any commotion. "What are your names?"

"I'm Peevy," said the first pale bat in a tone that sounded, well, peevish. "I'm the lead of the Pallid bat colony here."

"I'm Pushy," said the second pale bat in a gravelly voice that held no friendliness. "And this one leaning on me, here," Pushy tilted his head, "that's my Prickly."

"*Your* Prickly!" said the other Pallid bat mockingly. "You better be careful, Pushy, or I'll show you who's *your* boss around here!"

"OK, got it," said Volant trying to ignore the couple's tiff. "So there are two colonies in the cave then, right?"

"Yes, two colonies," said Prickly, turning to the eagle. "And we plan to keep it that way!" Prickly's tone was hot, as if steam might be coming off her head.

Volant looked down at the bat in confusion, unclear where her anger came from. Finally, Gabby piped in saying simply, "Huh?"

"Look, every year come late winter or early spring, meaning anytime now," Peevy took up the story, her voice also combative, "a colony of Long-nosed bats come across from the Mexican mainland. The rest of us live here all year, but those outsiders move with the blooming cactus."

"Interesting," Volant said.

"Not interesting, aggravating!" Pushy howled.

"Aggravating? Try infuriating!" shouted Prickly.

"Take it easy, you three," said Sully, with a tone indicating they'd been down this road before. Volant saw Sully's colony members—Sonar and Starr—both shift uncomfortably.

"The Long noses take nectar from the cactus flowers that we eat," stormed Peevy, giving Sully no heed. "Those cactus flowers rightfully belong to us!"

"How many total are you?" Volant asked, trying to steer the discussion onto a less controversial topic.

"About 2000 of us good-looking ones with the handsome noses," said Sully, the joke clearly an attempt to join Volant as a peacemaker. "I'd guess maybe 200 of our Pallid friends here."

Peevy nodded as if to say, "Yep, that sounds about right."

"The Long noses," Sully continued, "bring a really big cloud, but hard to guess a number as it varies with the year."

"Doesn't matter if it's ten or 100 or 10,000!" Peevy growled. "When they show up things get ugly fast. They're dirty and stupid and use resources that rightfully belong to us. The Long noses eat our food, for goodness sakes, *our* food!"

"What are you talking about, Peevy?" said Sully. "*Your* food? Pallids mostly eat scorpions, while the Long noses prefer nectar from cardón cactus."

"We eat from cardóns, too," Peevy shot back. "Maybe not as much, but it's our food, not theirs!"

"And not only that," shouted Pushy, picking up the story. "They try to take places in the cave that belong to us, then act like we owe it to them to provide them a home!"

"Calm down you two," Sully said.

"We won't calm down," snorted Pushy. "The Long noses change everything. They just don't fit in. Forget the noses. They also have tiny ears, so different from us Pallids and Leaf noses. They just don't belong here."

"I'm not so sure I agree." It was Starr, the dreamy Leaf-nosed bat. Her tone was kind and agreeable. Sully nodded his head as if to say, please, go ahead.

"It's not that big a deal, we can all co-exist," Starr said gently.

"Co-exist?" shouted Prickly, Pushy's steamed up companion, her voice acid. "With those tiny ears? Good Lord I can't bear to look at the ears on those bats! They're so...so *teensy-weensy*, they are just awful! I will not live with them."

Chapter 17

DURING THE NEXT month the birds and the bats did, as Volant had suggested, learn to live with each other. Everyday near sunset and sunrise Volant and Gabby would abandon the flat promontory to perch on the peak behind them or perhaps fly off somewhere to explore. That allowed the bats the freedom to fly in and out of their cave without interference.

That's not to say the bats and the birds didn't interact. Sully, the leader of the Leaf-nosed bats, and Volant the eagle began a friendship grounded in their shared love for flight. The two took to meeting on the peak at sunrise and sunset, as Sully was going to and coming from a night of hunting.

During one of those first meetings, as Volant and Sully were getting to know each other, Volant asked a question that had long intrigued her. "Why do you bats come out at night? Surely, it would be easier to see if you flew around during the day."

"Easier, maybe, but not as good," said Sully. "Night flying is far better for us bats. More insects are out at night, and a lot of us eat insects. Plus, lots of us use sound to locate our prey, so being able to see well in the dark is not critical. And at night, we don't have to compete for the insects with most of the birds who also eat insects. Oh, and some of the flowers we eat nectar from bloom at night so…"

"Ok, Ok, stop," said Volant, pretending to be overwhelmed. "Now I get it!"

"Good," chuckled Sully, "but there is one other thing worth mentioning. Sadly, some predators eat us bats, even eagles as we once discussed! Luckily for us, fewer predators are out at night. By the way, thanks once again for promising to focus on fish during your time in Baja!"

"Of course, friend," said Volant, eyes softening.

As the days went on, Sully and Volant more and more talked about what they'd seen and where they'd been on those marvelous flights that inspired them. Volant, for example, spoke of ten-foot tall grizzly bears in Alaska. "What?!" Sully exclaimed. "Is that possible? I've never been to Alaska—come to think of it I've never even seen a bear…of any kind!"

Sully, in turn, spoke of fish-eating bats that lived on the next island, just across the water. This time it was Volant's turn to say, "What?!" Volant turned her gaze to her diminutive friend and continued, "I thought you bats ate things like insects and plant nectar. How can a bat possibly catch fish to eat? Do the bats swim? Do they use little snorkels and spears?!"

"No, of course not," Sully chuckled. "They have big claws sort of like…well, sort of like *you* and use their claws to catch small fish just at the surface. Maybe I can introduce you to one of my fish-eating friends the next time they stop by. Who knows, maybe some night they'd let you fly along and observe while they hunt."

"I'd like that," said Volant, turning back to look up at a sky being colored by sunset. "Wow, so much to learn! Fish-eating bats, pale bats, bats with little ears, bats with long noses, bats with noses that look like leaves… Next thing you know, you're going to tell me there are bats that drink blood like vampires!"

"There are those, indeed, as well," said Sully.

"Oh come on," said Volant, looking to the sky incredulously. "For goodness sakes, Sully, now you're just pulling my talons. How many kinds of bats are there, anyways?"

"Many, my friend. More than you can count. Some even have wingspans as big as yours."

"OK, hold on my friend," said Volant. "There is no way that's possib…" Volant turned her face back to Sully for emphasis, only to find Sully was no longer there. Instead, Volant saw Sully 30 meters away, flying fast in pursuit of a fleeing moth.

Chapter 18

AS THE DAYS grew longer and warmer, the resident bats exiting and entering the cave largely forgot the birds. Peace settled comfortably onto the promontory and all seemed well with the world. Gabby the seagull had even made a new friend, a quirky osprey named Ollie, who was a bit in awe of Volant the eagle.

Then one day life on the island changed dramatically—the cloud of migrating Long-nosed bats arrived just before dawn!

Of course, the Long noses had been anticipated. For weeks Volant and Gabby heard Sonar the Leaf-nosed bat and Pushy the Pallid bat—the enforcement leads for their two colonies—talking about the arrival of the Long-nosed bats. Then, a week ago, they saw that Pushy had posted big-shouldered bats to patrol the cave border for the Pallid bats. Some of the guard bats hung from the tall cardón cactus that partially blocked the entrance to the cave; some guard bats hung along the edge of the cave entrance. The presence of these burly guards, along with the big cardón cactus, created a formidable boundary, a wall of sorts that could be used for controlling entry to the cave.

And for the Pallid bats controlling who could enter the cave was precisely the goal.

Chapter 19

THE EARLY MORNING that the Long-nosed bats arrived Gabby the seagull was not about. He had flown off with Ollie the osprey to explore a nearby island the evening before, saying he'd be back by dawn.

Volant the eagle rested on a far corner of the promontory. She was out of the way of the hordes of Leaf-nosed and Pallid bats returning to the cave, but near enough to make out the figures of Sonar, Pushy, and dozens of enforcement sentries, each working a checkpoint, and to hear their talk.

The Long-nosed swarm winged off the sea and over the island as the sky to the east lightened. The Long noses flew in a blocky formation having the silhouette of an extended caravan. Once over the island, the big group of bats—looking to include far more members than the Pallids or even the Leaf noses—quickly amassed above the promontory, near the cave entrance. But there they hesitated, intimidated by the guards yelling at them to go away even as scores of Leaf-nosed and Pallid bats glided by and into the cave. Two bats from those passing—

Starr the Leaf nosed and Prickly the Pallid—dropped out of swarms entering to land near the cave entrance.

Volant heard weary groans from the caravan of Long-nosed bats, and could see some of them struggling to stay in the air. Pandemonium reigned.

Long moments ticked by until finally three of the Long noses dropped to hover in front of the cardón cactus, sticking their extended noses into flowers to collect nectar. In an instant, a small force of bat guards set upon them. Pushy, who was in the lead, scared them off shouting, "Go away you Long noses! We don't want you here!"

"That's right—you're not welcome here!" yelled Peevy to the three fleeing bats.

"Wait," said Starr timidly, "they're not hurting…"

But Starr was cut off. Peevy, who had raised her eyes higher to the swarm of Long-nosed bats circling the cave, drowned Starr out yelling, "None of you invaders belong here!"

"That's right," Prickly screamed, joining the din. "This is *our* land, this is *our* food!"

Chapter 20

FOR A SHORT time the swarm of Long-nosed bats lifted away from the cave entrance, forming a bubble of sorts over the promontory. But hunger and fatigue soon proved too strong and when Gabby the seagull returned and landed close by on the promontory, a lone Long-nosed bat took advantage of the interruption and dropped down from the swarm to hover in front of the cactus.

"Please, you must help us!" cried the Long-nosed bat to the imposing bats patrolling the cave boundary. When there was no response, the Long nose turned to the apparent security leaders, Sonar and Pushy, who were out front, and pleaded, "Please! We flew across the sea tonight. We are tired and hungry. Many of our females are pregnant, weak, and barely hanging on!"

Before the bats could answer, Gabby chimed in, drawing everyone's attention. "I can verify that. Ollie and I saw the Long-nosed swarm crossing the sea, but sadly some of their lot had fallen from the sky and were clinging to rafts of seaweed and logs. I'm guessing they won't make it."

"Oh, no," said Starr, the Leaf-nosed bat.

Peevy, Pushy, and Prickly, the Pallid bats, grunted as one, looking irritated and unmoved.

But Sonar the Leaf-nosed security lead softened, looking back to the Long-nosed bat and saying, "Who are you and how many are you? Why are you here?"

"My name is Lepto," said the Long nose. "We are Long-nosed bats, perhaps 5000 in our swarm. But please, you know who we are and why we are here. Every year we follow the Nectar Trail, northward from Mexico and later back again. We keep moving to new locations where plants are flowering, including cactus like the cardón."

"There is nothing for us on the Mexican mainland now," Lepto continued with passion. "The opportunity is *here*; the cardón are beginning to bloom *here*. We only need a place to stay and rest up, and some food and water. We are just trying to get to the peninsula for food and for a place for our pregnant mothers, including me, to give birth. Please, can you help us? Can we share your cave?"

Pushy looked ready to explode, but just as he drew a breath for the outburst, another Long-nosed bat cried out, "Yes, please help us!"

This second Long nose arrived from *behind* the guards, making it clear that it had somehow gotten into the cave and had just now exited. Pushy and

Peevy turned as one to give the bat guards behind them angry looks.

"My name is Luna," said the new Long-nosed bat, oblivious to the hostility on display. "My grandparents recall staying in this cave years back. They said it would be perfect for our group's travels."

"Things have changed," said Pushy. "We don't want your kind here."

"We are full up," Prickly added. "There is no more room."

"But that's not true," said Luna, looking at Lepto and then back to the leaders. "I was just in the cave and it is enormous. It's big enough to hold us all."

"It is *exactly* big enough to hold the Leaf noses and the Pallids, and no one but those," snarled Peevy. "We don't like your weird, teeny ears. We don't like the way you look."

"Oh please," said Lepto, desperate, "just a few nights while we rest."

"No!" It was Pushy again. "You eat from the cardóns—that is *our* food!"

"Please, have a heart," said Luna. "Just a few nights and then we can move on to find more cardóns on the peninsula. Please, there is space and opportunity for all."

"What do you not understand about *our*? It is *our* food!" cried Prickly.

"Hold on," said Lepto. "We also pollinate cactus so that *new* cardóns grow that we can *all* eat. We do important work, and we do it everywhere we go. If it wasn't for us there might not be any cardóns for anyone, including the Leaf noses and the Pallids!"

"Oh please," sneered Peevy. "How many times and in how many ways do we have to say that your kind are not welco…"

But Peevy didn't get out the rest of her words. Volant the eagle, who had hopped closer, suddenly interrupted saying, "Hold it, who is that?"

The bats, whose eyes aren't as good as an eagle's, turned to follow Volant's gaze to the east. It took a moment for the object of Volant's attention to materialize for the rest of them as a faint outline against the lightening sky.

Then, Gabby said, "Wait, what? Another swarm of bats?"

In moments, the bat swarm, looking similar in size to the already hovering Long noses, was upon the promontory. Immediately, two bats from the new swarm swooped down out of the sky. These bats, like the others in the new swarm, had long tails, unlike any of the other bats present. But the new bats also had big-ish ears, far more like the big ears of the Leaf noses and the Pallids than the small ones of the Long noses.

A couple of the new bats swooped in and settled onto the cardón cactus, one of them promptly announcing, "My name is Flow, and this is Swift— she is also from our colony. We're Free-tailed bats."

The bats introduced themselves around, as did Volant. Gabby did likewise, adding, "*Fastest Flier in the Sky!*" as a prideful endnote. Volant thought she noticed the new bat Swift wince at Gabby's bragging statement.

"We're heading back to Texas," Flow said, after the introductions. "It's a long ways, and our group is worn to the bone and in need of a place to rest and recuperate. We are wondering if we might stay in your...."

But before Flow completed her question, Peevy waved the new bats and their swarm into the bat cave, and indicated to the guards to let them pass. Pushy and Prickly nodded their agreement.

"What?!" yelled Lepto and Luna, the Long-nosed bats, in unison. "Those bats aren't Leaf noses or Pallids—why did you let them in and not us?!"

Chapter 21

AS QUICKLY AS the Free-tailed bats, Flow and Swift, and their Free-tailed compatriots disappeared into the cave, yelling started anew between Long-nosed and Pallid bats. But soon another voice, the biggest voice, interrupted again.

"Excuse me, everyone," said Volant the eagle. "I know I'm also pretty new here at the bat cave, but I have an idea. Will you listen?"

The bats, all of them, looked between themselves. No one need say that Volant was a giant among them—with a sharp beak and talons, to boot—and the fact she was new here, and not even a bat, thus had little bearing.

"What then?" said Peevy, irritated.

"Sully's not back from hunting, but he told me that there is another cave that..."

At that moment, Sully the Leaf-nosed leader slipped out of the sky. "Wrong my friend, I *am* back," Sully said to Volant. Then, to everyone, "What is happening here? I see the Long noses have arrived—I just flew through them. Why are they circling there instead of going into the cave? And didn't I see some Free tails just head inside?"

"You know exactly why the Long noses aren't allowed!" shouted Peevy. "They are villains and criminals, every one of them, and..."

"... and they eat our food and they have those tiny ears," Prickly interrupted, taking up the attack. "They DO NOT belong here!"

"Oh, not *this* again," lamented Sully. And then, looking to Volant, "Almost every year."

"You're the leader," Volant said, focused on Sully alone. "Can't you just let them into the cave?"

"Yes, can't we?" pleaded Starr the dreamy Leaf nose. "What about the expectant mothers?"

"I can't...we can't," said Sully, with a sad nod to Starr. Then, with a look back to Volant, Sully said, "True, the Pallids are just a small group. But they are loud and so easy to anger and the simple fact is that we have to live with them the rest of the year. They despise the Long noses in part because they eat from the cardóns that the Pallids also love. Sure, we Leaf noses mostly eat insects, but we sometimes eat from the cardóns, too. And we're willing to share with the Long noses when they pass through."

"That sounds reasonable," said Volant.

"But not to the Pallids," continued Sully. "The Pallids seem to accept the Free tails, but just hate the Long noses because of...well I'm not sure, but along with fighting the Long nose for the cardóns, it seems like it's because those tiny ears make them different."

"Hmm," mumbled Volant, clearly disturbed by Sully's comments.

"In some years" Sully continued, "the Long noses have made it all the way across to the peninsula without needing to stop on the island. But looks like this won't be one of those lucky years."

"Hold on a second," said Volant, her tone brightening. "I was just about to say that you once told me there's another, unconnected cave down at the water's edge. Could that cave work for the Long noses?"

"Ah, yes, good memory," replied Sully. "That cave's a bit damp with the ocean waves splashing in, and pretty filthy and cramped. Far better would be for the Long noses to join the rest of us in the main cave."

"Over my dead body!" snapped Pushy, breaking into the discussion.

Sonar, the Leaf-nosed security lead, gave his boss Sully a look and a shrug that said, "I sorta agree with you, but I also kinda agree with Pushy. Regardless, the Long noses are *no way* going into the main cave."

Seeing the looks that passed between Sully and Sonar, Volant broke the silence, offering, "How about the Long noses use the other cave? It's only temporary—would that be possible?"

"We should really be able to do better than that; the Long noses are bats, too," said Sully. Then, making his decision, Sully said, "But as you say, Volant, it's only temporary, so I think that would work."

Starr beamed; Prickly scowled. Sonar nodded in agreement, relieved he would not have to go against the wishes of the Pallid bats.

Lepto and Luna looked on expectantly, now turning their gazes to Peevy and Pushy and Prickly....

Silence.

When the silence became uncomfortable, Volant bent, her intimidating mass hovering above the three Pallid bats, and for the first time ever seen by the bats, menace came into the eagle's yellow eyes.

Quickly Peevy allowed, "Ok...for one night..."

Volant leaned over further, glaring.

"Ok maybe two nights, but that's it, nothing more!" When Volant's eyes moved to Pushy, the bat nodded his agreement, slipping ever so slightly back behind his partner Prickly, who continued to scowl defiantly, but stayed quiet.

"Thank you," said Luna.

"Yes, thank you," said a relieved Lepto. "Our colony is desperate. We are tired and we are hungry. Thank you for this little bit of hope. We *must* stay somewhere."

IT ONLY TOOK the Long-nosed bat swarm 20 minutes to settle into the lower cave. The remaining Leaf-nosed and Pallid bats had retired to the upper cave, which now included the Free tails from Texas, as well.

At last, Volant and Gabby sat alone on the promontory. But unlike the usual quiet of sunrise, from below came new sounds: sighs of relief mingling with groans of disgust as the Long noses settled into their sub-par cave.

Chapter 22

THE LONG NOSES stayed for two days. When they ventured out that next night they did not find a welcome greeting. Instead, Pallid bats—plus a few Leaf-nosed bats—harassed and dive-bombed them for sipping nectar from cardóns on the island. So instead, the Long noses flew to the nearby island, where they found far fewer cardóns and barely enough food for the night.

The newly arrived Free tails, who ate mostly insects, went about their business undisturbed. With no one pushing them to leave, Flow the Free-tailed bat leader talked with her compatriot Swift and decided their swarm would stay longer, as the Free tails were in great need of rest.

ON THEIR SECOND night, the Long-nosed bat swarm lifted off and pointed itself to the peninsula. The last to leave were Lepto and Luna. They found Volant the eagle and Sully the Leaf-nose leader talking on the promontory, as was their habit before Sully took off to hunt for the night. Flow the Free-tailed leader was perched nearby, watching.

"Thank you for helping us," said Lepto to Volant and Sully.

"Yes, thank you," said Luna.

"Of course," replied Volant.

"I only wish we could have done more," said Sully.

Chapter 23

WITHIN A FEW days of the Long-nosed bats' departure, Flow the Free-tailed bat leader started joining Volant the eagle and Sully the Leaf-nosed leader at dusk, before the bat swarms headed out to find food.

Volant and Sully brought Flow into the discussions of their shared joys of flight and travel and the oddities of the world. At first, they repeated stories for Flow of things they'd already covered: Alaskan grizzly bears and fish-eating bats and more. Later the focus of their talks changed, with Volant and Sully asking Flow about the Free tails and their travels.

"I've never been to Texas," Volant said. "Maybe some other winter."

"Nor have the Leaf noses," said Sully, "and doubt we ever will. But yes, I'd love to hear about it!"

Flow told Volant and Sully amazing stories about how BIG Texas is, with BIG cities filled with people, and then, "In one town there's a BIG bridge where we bats roost. But we bats aren't the only ones there. People swarm around the bridge just to see us come and go. Every sunset the place transforms from peaceful to chaotic! It's kind of a party!"

ONE EVENING FLOW'S Free-tailed compatriot Swift dropped in and joined the discussion of the three regulars. That night Flow was describing the Free tails onward travels. "We'll point straight at Texas," Flow said. "It's a long haul, but once we get to Texas we end our travels at the BIGGEST cave anyone could ever imagine!"

Swift nodded in agreement. "It's HUGE!" she beamed.

"And there are millions of bats!" exclaimed Flow.

Sully's eyes grew wide, trying to imagine it all, but Volant jumped in skeptically, saying, "Oh come on, now. That must just be another Texas tale. Surely there couldn't be mill…"

Suddenly a blur of white crash-landed on the promontory, stopping the conversation and almost wiping out the eagle and three bats. It was Gabby the seagull, returning from a day of exploring with his friend, Ollie the Osprey.

"Whoa, slow down Gabby! You're going to hurt someone," chastised Volant.

"Sorry, sorry, everyone," said Gabby. "But doggone it's hard for me to slow down. I am, after all, *The Fastest Flier in the Sky!*"

"Argh," said Flow, having by now heard Gabby make this claim several times. "I'm guessing Swift here," she nodded to her Free-tailed compatriot, "might have something to say about that whole *Fastest Flier in the Sky* thing."

"Indeed I might," said Swift, giving a flip of her tail while looking Gabby up and down.

"Harrumph," said Gabby, unimpressed.

Chapter 24

FOR SEVERAL WEEKS life on the promontory skipped along in a peaceful, quiet manner, temperatures slowly increasing. Actually, that's not quite all true. The peace and quiet was interrupted twice a day when the bats left the cave to go out to gather food at dusk, then returned near sunrise.

Oh, and there was something else neither peaceful nor quiet: Every day when the bats took flight Gabby the seagull and Swift the Free-tailed bat squabbled. They'd had it in for each other ever since the day Gabby had crash-landed on the promontory and then boldly claimed to be *The Fastest Flier in the Sky*.

"You're slower than a starfish!" Swift yelled as she buzzed Gabby just after popping out of the cave one evening. "You want to see *The Fastest Flier in the Sky*? Try this on for fast!" Swift did a loop around Gabby that made the seagull's head spin.

"Fast, my eye!" Gabby yelled after Swift, trying to appear unimpressed. "You couldn't outrace a tortoise with a broken leg!"

Day after day the bickering continued. "You're nothing but a sea horse!"

"I'd rather be that than a manatee like you!"

Witnessing the nearly nightly melee, Volant, Sully, and Flow would share a collective shrug of the shoulders, and then a grin.

DURING ONE OF the talks between Volant and her two bat friends, Flow mentioned something peculiar. "The big cave where we live in Texas—remember the one I told you has millions of bats?—has mostly us Free tails, but it also has a few other bat species. And among them we saw something really odd last year."

"Odd? What do you mean by *odd*?" asked Volant.

"Last year," Flow continued, "Swift told me she landed for the night on the edge of our colony. One of the bats in the colony next to us had a bizarre look: some sort of white powder on its nose. Swift tried to ask the bat what the white powder was, but she said the bat couldn't answer, it was just sort of lethargic."

"That is weird," said Sully. "I've never seen a bat like that here in Baja."

"But that wasn't the weirdest—or the saddest—thing," said Flow. "Swift said once the bat left the cave in the middle of the day, flying erratically."

"Flying erratically? In broad daylight? What on Earth?" said Sully.

"Indeed, exactly what I said," returned Flow. Then, looking to Volant, she added, "We bats don't like going out in the daylight, it's too dangerous."

Volant, who had been listening intently, nodded her head as if to indicate she was aware of that fact. Then the big eagle turned her head away, thinking, a troubled look coming into her eyes. Volant recalled the bat she and Gabby had seen in California, the one that flew in a wobbly fashion at, strangely, mid-morning. Volant decided not to say anything about the incident to her bat friends, but suddenly the eagle's stomach felt uneasy.

Chapter 25

IN THE DARK of night a week later, Volant the eagle watched from the promontory as a boat, heralded by its running lights, approached. As the boat came to shore five headlamps popped on, providing enough light for Volant to see that it was the same people who had come to the island weeks back, though with someone new.

The people climbed out of their old scarred boat. They unloaded backpacks, coolers, and gear, including what looked like a rolled up net and some pillowcases. All the gear on shore, the people put on full-body white suits. Most of that matched their first visit to the island, Volant noted, but this time, something different: This time they had far more gear, and the new person had a dog—an overly rambunctious, tail-wagging, nose-to-the-ground, sniff-sniff-sniffing mutt!

Something else was different, Volant quickly noticed. On this trip, the group did not disappear below the promontory. Instead, they climbed toward it. When it became apparent that the group—and that pesky dog!—were heading straight for her,

Volant took flight, heading off the back side of the promontory. Volant heard the dog whine, but nothing else that indicated the people might be aware of her departure.

Volant flew high above the island, circling time and again in hopes of learning what the people were doing. It wasn't long before she saw them arrive at the promontory. They paused to sort through gear near the big cardón cactus, put on masks, gloves, and booties, and then one-by-one disappeared into the cave, each person turning sideways as they shimmied in through the entrance. The second to the last to enter was the dog, now on a leash, whining, nose to the ground, intent on something.

Chapter 26

VOLANT CIRCLED THE island for an hour, wondering what was happening in the bat cave. As the sun became a hint below the horizon, the bats—first a few, then by the hundreds upon hundreds—arrived back at the promontory and slipped into the cave.

An hour later, with the sun fully showing, Gabby the seagull returned from a visit with Ollie the osprey to a nearby island. Gabby joined Volant in the air. The two friends flew in tandem for a time, enjoying an effortless glide off the day's first thermals coming up from the island.

Eventually, Gabby said, "I love soaring Volant, just like you! But Ollie and I saw you an hour ago doing the same thing. What's up? Why are you just circling the island? We might as well go land."

"We can't," came Volant's reply and Gabby heard an uneasy edge in the eagle's voice.

"Why not?" Gabby asked.

"The people we saw weeks ago—remember them?—are back," Volant said.

Gabby nodded that he did remember, saying, "Yes they splashed and giggled in the…"

"No, not that group. The others," said Volant, "the ones that wore white suits and disappeared under the promontory."

"Oh yes, them. That was weird," said Gabby. "I've always wondered what they were doing."

"I'm starting to wonder if they went into the same cave where the Long-nosed bats stayed," Volant said. "Because today they climbed to the promontory and then dropped into the main bat cave. They're in there now."

"What!" exclaimed Gabby.

"There's more," continued Volant. "They have a dog."

"A dog! On the island?!" shouted Gabby, now truly alarmed. Gabby, like Volant, was no fan of dogs.

Chapter 27

THROUGH THE DAY Volant the eagle and Gabby the seagull circled the promontory, waiting, watching. They worried for their bat friends. Several times they saw one or two people come out of the cave to deposit something in the cooler, or to take off their mask and gloves, get a drink, and stretch. But always the people would don their gear again and head right back into the cave.

When Volant and Gabby got tired circling they took turns dropping to the palapa on the beach, the one they had perched on their first night on the island. Gabby was there late in the afternoon when the five people and the dog all exited the cave, this time with a look of finality.

Gabby quickly took flight to join Volant as the people dropped equipment and six small cages near the cave entrance, where they'd earlier left two coolers. Hoping to keep the dog from overheating, the new man tied it to the larger cooler in the shade of the big cardón, then poured the dog some water.

The five set about labeling, sorting, and storing vials and jars into the big cooler, working around the dog. Four of them lifted the cages, peered into them, made notes in notebooks and stuck a label on each cage. One man took photo after photo. Tasks complete, the people put each cage just inside the cave.

As they circled high above, Volant, her voice uneasy, said, "Gabby, did you hear the chirps and screeches?"

"No," said Gabby looking straight into Volant's troubled eyes. "You mean like our bat friends make?"

"Yes, *exactly* like that," said Volant. "And then the sounds disappeared when they put the cages back in the cave. I think they captured some of the bats— I'm sure I heard Sonar and Starr and others."

"Oh no!" said Gabby.

The seagull turned his eyes back to the promontory in time to see the five people strip off their masks, gloves, and white suits and stow them into backpacks. "Wait," Gabby said, "what are they doing now? Are they done in the cave?"

Volant and Gabby watched as the people set the backpacks aside, opened the smaller cooler, grabbed cold drinks and some food, and collapsed on the promontory. A less business-like banter began. One man, who they could now see looked older than the rest, continued taking photos of the other four and the dog after they were all settled on the ground.

Volant and even Gabby could see that the five were worn out. "They look happier than last we saw them," Gabby said, "like maybe they accomplished something this time."

"Agree, perhaps," said Volant. "But even so, something doesn't look right. A couple of them look troubled."

"Really?" said Gabby. "I guess I can't see that as well as you. But hey, why don't I go down there and find out what's going on? I'll just pretend I'm looking for food."

Before Volant could remark on the intelligence of such a move, Gabby dove for the promontory, and a few moments later made an awkward, noisy landing.

Chapter 28

AT GABBY THE seagull's appearance, the dog popped up, barking. But the new man, who wore a short-brimmed cycling cap and worked with the dog almost exclusively, said, "Batey, quiet down. You don't need to protect us. It's just a seagull. You've done your work for the day."

"Too true," said a woman in a no-nonsense tone. The woman wore an orange ball cap, below which a short, tight ponytail showed. Even from afar, Volant the eagle had correctly identified her as the group's leader. And her expression was, indeed, troubled as she looked to the dog and said, "You may have found us something we've dreaded ever finding, Batey."

"That it wasn't so," returned a second man who wore thick, heavily framed glasses. He and the woman exchanged a grave look that spoke legions. Then he turned his focus to the man wearing the cycling cap, saying, "Happy with one result of today's work: Batey never signaled that he'd found COVID in the cave. But not so happy with the idea he might have found the fungus."

"Wait," said a second, younger woman, before the man with the cap could respond. The younger woman had a nose stud and wore a blue baseball cap, in her case backwards. She was sitting next to Batey and as she reached down to scratch the dog's ears said, "I thought Batey's ability to smell disease was just an experiment."

"Yes, that's what I thought, too," said the older man, for once lowering his camera.

"Well, sort of," said the man with the cycling cap. "To smell the fungus that causes White-nose Syndrome is, yes, experimental. But we know for certain that Batey, and other dogs, can detect COVID, cancer, many diseases. We've proven that time and again."

"How do they do it?" asked the younger woman. "How do they detect disease?"

"The big thing is a dog doesn't necessarily *detect disease* directly," answered the man with the cycling cap. "Instead they might be detecting the pathogen that causes a disease—like looking for the fungus as we were doing today—or they might be detecting scents from metabolic changes caused by a disease. Those scents might show up as changes in the breath or urine or feces or…"

"Oh, I see," said the younger woman, eyes lighting up. "So the dog can smell those changes and thus, sorta, smell disease. Cool!"

"Yes, fascinating!" said the man with the thick glasses. "Still, let's backtrack. It takes time— right?—to train a dog to detect each new and specific disease…or, as you say, pathogen that causes a disease…or new scents caused by metabolic changes. And you've only just begun training Batey to detect the fungus we're interested in. So as she said," here he nodded to the younger woman, "today's work is just an experiment so…."

"…so we can't be sure," said the man with the cycling cap, completing the thought. "True and yes, dogs can be fallible, of course. But even given our limited training runs, Batey proved pretty accurate in detecting the fungus. That's why I offered that we add the fungus detection as part of our work with you on looking for COVID, Batey's bread and butter."

"Still," said the woman with the orange cap, "it *is* never-before-done work. So let's hope Batey is wrong."

"Agreed, it's all new," said the man with the cycling cap. "But here's the bottom line: I long ago learned that it's a good bet to *always* trust the dog's nose."

The woman in the orange cap grimaced.

Chapter 29

GABBY THE SEAGULL, who'd been listening from a discrete distance to the people's banter, heard Volant the eagle call from above. Not wanting to leave, Gabby sent up her own squawk, which caused Batey to jump up, straining at his tether and whining.

"Batey, I told you to settle down," said the man with the cycling cap. The dog obeyed, tongue lolling, eyes intent on Gabby.

"C'mon Batey," said the younger woman with the nose stud and blue ball cap, reaching out again to scratch the dog's ears. "Quiet down boy. Forget about the seagull. It won't hurt us; it's just here to beg for food."

As Batey whined, the man with the cycling cap turned his attention back to the woman in the orange cap and the man in the thick glasses, saying, "This work has been super exciting to try once—thanks again to you both for inviting me. If we're ever to make this an ongoing research practice, far better for our dogs to go in and detect scents that indicate pathogens or disease in the scat when the bats are away from the cave, or that we bring the scat out to the dogs so they don't have to go into the cave. Even in those cases we'd need to be diligent, like today and in the days ahead, to confirm the dog doesn't get sick from the very diseases it is trying to detect."

The woman with the orange ball cap nodded in agreement, then said, "Fully understood and agreed regarding the importance of taking care of the dogs. Animal welfare is paramount, be it working dogs or wild bats. But today's work is admittedly unique for us: both the experiment with Batey as a detection dog and getting permitted to take bats back to our lab for mist vaccine studies."

Here the man in the glasses picked up the thought, saying, "Yes, on the latter front I am really hopeful the misting will provide a way to introduce vaccines that can interrupt the process of disease transmission."

"Detecting disease and stopping disease transmission—both are clearly critically important," said the man with the cycling cap. "Regardless of whether it's White-nose Syndrome within bat populations, or myriad diseases like COVID spilling over from bats to humans…"

"…or humans to bats, let's not forget, like we're testing for," interrupted the man with the thick glasses.

"… or COVID moving from humans to bats," smiled the man with the biking cap.

"It's all big stuff," said the woman in the orange cap. "And of course we won't know until we know."

As the man in the heavy glasses nodded in agreement, the woman with the orange ball cap turned to the man with the cycling cap, and said, "Whether yes or no on the fungus detection, again, our great, great thanks to you and Batey and the scent-training effort your folks put in back home. Your willingness to collaborate with us for several weeks is a great benefit to our research."

"And *your* willingness to have us join you is a great benefit to *our* work and knowledge, as well," said the man in the cycling cap. He tipped the cap's brim and gave the woman in the orange ball cap a smile, which she returned.

Then, eyes lighting up with a bit of mischief, the woman said, "We'll find out once we're back in the lab whether we can *always trust the dog's nose*."

The man with the cycling cap said nothing but instead rolled his eyes in false drama, as if used to hearing such healthy—though regularly proven wrong—skepticism.

Then Batey, oblivious to all the talk about his abilities, jumped up again, intent on Gabby, who had been sneaking ever closer.

"Batey, down!" said the man with the cycling cap. The dog obeyed, tongue lolling, eyes intent on Gabby.

The younger woman turned and shooed Gabby away, but not so far he couldn't hear the people's continuing conversation.

Chapter 30

WITH THE SUN just touching the horizon, the people climbed back to the peak for their last trip to shuttle cages, coolers, and gear back to the boat. On the promontory, the younger woman with the blue ball cap on backwards untied Batey from the big cooler. The dog immediately jumped at Gabby, almost pulling the woman over and sending the seagull, squawking wildly, into the air. The man with the cycling cap signaled the straining younger woman, and she handed him the leash.

It took a few minutes for Gabby to climb high enough to join up with Volant.

"What's going on down there?" asked the eagle as the two friends circled together.

"You mean aside from me getting attacked by a vicious dog?" said Gabby. "I'm fine, thanks for asking!"

Volant waited, unmoved.

"Oh my, oh my, a lot was going on down there!" Gabby said in a voice of equal parts excitement and dread. "And it's not goo...."

"Hold that thought," Volant interrupted. "The boat is pushing off and I just realized the bats should be coming out any second. Let's get down to the promontory and find out from Sully and Flow what happened in the cave. You can tell me what you heard later."

Gabby pulled up short, surprised at Volant's abrupt change of heart, but could say nothing since the eagle had already dived to the promontory. With a shrug, Gabby pursued.

By the time the two birds landed, the boat had motored away toward the peninsula. An orange glow settled beyond the departing boat, while purples colored the eastern sky.

Bats began to emerge from the cave. Among the first out were the two leaders, Sully of the Leaf-nosed bats and Flow of the Free-tailed bats. "Are you two OK?" asked Volant before the two bats had even settled. "What happened in there?"

"Yes, tell us!" exclaimed Gabby. "Out here on the promontory the people kept talking about *COVID* this and *fungus and syndrome* that."

"No, we are not OK," said Sully, ignoring Gabby and addressing Volant. "They put up a net and caught some of our bat friends as we all came back into the cave this morning. They put six of our friends into cages—Leaf noses, Pallids, and Free tails. One of the Leaf noses was Sonar, our security lead! And Starr, too! The people just snatched all of them from the cave." Sully, face downtrodden, fell silent thinking of his Leaf-nosed friends.

"And they got Pushy and Prickly, too," said Peevy angrily.

"I am so sorry," said Volant, head tilted. "I could hear them chirping back and forth at each other after their cages were carried to the promontory."

"There's more," said Flow, disgust in her voice as she picked up the story. "They put some of the bats they captured into white sacks and gassed them! Then they swabbed their skin, and stuck needles into them and collected their blood in vials!"

"They did what?" asked Volant, aghast. "How frightening that must have been!"

"No more frightening than that dog!" exclaimed Sully, jumping back into the conversation. "It raced around the cave, nose to the ground or to the cave walls smelling everything. It seemed possessed. But then, strangely, sometimes the dog suddenly stopped and sat and stared with wild eyes, its tail flying back and forth. Whenever that happened one of the people would come over and scratch its ears. Then they would run a swab along the cave wall, or scrape some soil off the cave floor and put whatever they collected into a bottle."

Volant's brow furrowed, eyes narrowing. "How incredibly strange that sounds, Sully. But *why* were the people there? And *what* was that dog doing?"

Sully looked to Flow, shaking his head as if to say, you go ahead.

"We don't know," said Flow. "But there's even something worse! Sometimes the dog sniffed a cluster of us bats on the cave wall. Most of the time it would move on, but a couple of times it stopped, whined, and fixated on a group of bats as if it was pointing out something. Every time that happened, one of the people would come forward to inspect the roosting bats. They looked like ghosts with their white costumes and lights on their heads…"

"…and several times they grabbed one of our friends off the wall!" interjected Sully.

"That must have been so unnerving!" said Volant. "And it makes no sense."

"Unnerving, indeed!" said Gabby, who had been listening to the back and forth. "But it might make sense—at least I think so because it all sorta fits with what I saw out on the promontory, and what the people were saying."

For the first time since Sully and Flow had come out of the cave, all eyes turned to Gabby.

Chapter 31

"THE DOG CAN do what? Oh come on!" said Volant the eagle after Gabby the seagull began recounting the discussions he heard between the people.

"I'm telling you," said Gabby defensively, "they said the dog can smell disease. I know, it sounds crazy, but that's what they said."

"And they said there's a disease in the bat cave...," Sully the Leaf-nosed bat leader, started to ask.

"...and some of the bats have it?" Flow the Free-tailed leader interrupted, piling onto Sully's question.

"No ... well, yes ... well *two* diseases ... well no ... well, doggone it, I don't know!" said Gabby, exasperated. "They said there *might* be disease in the cave. They seemed really worried. They kept talking about how people can give the bats something called *COVID* and how bad that would be because even if the bats don't get sick they can pass it on to other animals or right back to people later. And also they talked about a fungus and white noses and feeble bats and bats flying off-kilter and about how bat colonies around the world have been wiped out."

"Oh no!" said Sully and Flow at once.

"But then they said they didn't think there was any way that the disease that causes the bats to have white noses, they called it a *syndrome*," continued Gabby, "could come to Baja, because it was too warm here—at least out here on the islands—and that to get the White-nose Syndrome the bats needed to catch it from a fungus while they were hibernating, because when they hibernate their immune systems are a bit suppressed making them especially susceptible to…"

"Slow down, Gabby!" said Volant. "This is a lot to take in all at once."

"I know it is and I don't even remember it all," said Gabby. "But I do remember the older woman, the one with the orange ball cap, saying how the fungus causes the disease and that if the fungus makes it here to Baja, even if it doesn't cause disease here, it could move on to other places where bats do hibernate, possibly causing White-nose Syndrome there and killing more bats."

"That's terrible!" exclaimed Sully.

"Really disturbing!" added Flow.

"Yes, disturbing for the people, too," concluded Gabby. "That last idea stopped their discussion cold.

They all just sat there for a time, saying nothing more, looking worried."

At this turn in Gabby's story, Sully, Flow, and Volant looked worried themselves. Everyone quieted, unsure of what to make of Gabby's report.

AFTER A LONG period, Gabby finally broke the silence, saying quietly, "I guess I'm just not sure what it all means."

"I think what it means," said Volant, brow furrowed and eyes aglow, "is that we need to be concerned." Volant looked at Sully and Flow and continued, "In California, Gabby and I saw a dazed bat one morning long after the rest of the bats had settled for the day. That bat flew all off-kilter, just like the people said, and it didn't look one bit healthy."

Gabby nodded that he, too, remembered that bat.

"But I'm not sure if it had a white nose," Volant said. "And I've never seen a bat with a white nose here. Have you Sully? Have you Flow?"

"No, I never have. Not here, not anywhere," said Sully, perplexed.

"No, me neither, not here," said Flow, speaking slowly, dread in her voice. "But unfortunately I *have* seen bats with white noses before: once in New

Mexico on our way through, and a bunch back home in Texas. Remember, Volant? I told you about it a while ago."

Volant nodded that she remembered.

Flow continued for the benefit of others, "Last year some bats in Texas got white noses and then they got really sick while they were hibernating. It woke them up sometimes. They lost weight and got all lethargic."

"That doesn't sound good," said Sully.

"It wasn't," Flow continued. "Sadly, most of those bats eventually died. We didn't know what to do to help them."

Chapter 32

DAYS PASSED, THEN a week, then two weeks. Life changed. While worries about the captured bats remained, worries about the five people and the question of white noses were largely set aside. The length of the days began to change dramatically, and more and more Flow the Free-tailed leader talked about the need for the Free tails to make a change themselves. It was getting closer to the time for them to migrate back to Texas.

One thing had not changed: the squabbling between Gabby the seagull and Swift the Free-tailed bat. On and on it went, usually with Volant the eagle, Sully the Leaf-nose leader, and Flow the Free-tailed leader, looking on in amusement. Each sunset they watched thousands of bats peacefully emerge from the cave and go on their merry way. But then the fireworks always started when Swift appeared and bombed down on Gabby.

"You couldn't outrun a sleeping koala!" shouted Swift.

"Really? Is that the best you got Ms. Loris?" returned Gabby.

Finally, after weeks of this silliness, Volant, Sully, and Flow waved for the two turbo-charged egos to stop their bickering and join them.

"We've been talking," said Volant, "and wonder why you two don't just race and settle this nonsense once and for all?"

"Yes," Sully concurred. "Aside from our missing friends, you two and your bickering is about all the bats in the cave talk about anymore."

"A race?" Gabby said, as if for the first time considering the possibility. "Where?"

"Sully, Volant, and I were thinking to the town on the peninsula," said Flow. "Say from the promontory here over to the lighthouse at the marina."

Sully and Volant nodded in agreement.

"And the winner is declared *The Fastest Flier in the Sky*?" asked Swift.

"Indeed he or she will be," said Sully.

"Well I'm in! You in, ya little snail?" said Gabby, scowling down at Swift.

"Oh, you bet I'm in," said Swift, glaring right back up at Gabby. "I'm *all* in, ya big sloth!"

Chapter 33

IT WAS A week later, and finally sunset on the day of the big race had arrived. Both Gabby the seagull and Swift the Free-tailed bat had made multiple practice runs to the town on the peninsula and back that week. Both brimmed with confidence as they waited on the promontory, Gabby perched at the highest point, Swift hanging upside down just below.

Bats from the cave—Leaf noses, Pallids, and Free tails—emerged from the cave early that evening, all wanting to see the race. Even several of the fish-eating bats from the next island were in attendance. The bats flitted and circled and swarmed over the peak, all yelling encouragement for Swift.

"Too bad, so sad Swift, that you'll be disappointing all your friends tonight," said Gabby.

"No way, Gab-ster," snorted Swift. "You're going down hard. And by the way, at least *I* have some friends!"

True, Gabby realized, his stomach suddenly raw. While word of the big race had filtered through the bird world, none of the pelicans, boobies, or gulls who said they'd show up were present. Not even his oddball osprey friend, Ollie, was there. Ollie told Gabby he himself should be in the race, but given he wasn't invited, he'd come to cheer the seagull on saying, "We birds will show that cheeky bat Swift, and *all* the bats, a thing or two!"

But looking about, Gabby saw no Ollie. Instead, he returned his attention to Swift, who continued her rant, "...and you know what else? You are nothing more than a Spruce Goose!"

"OK, first off," said Gabby, trying to get back on track, "I have *lots* of friends, including Volant and Ollie and pelicans and even goose frien...." But Gabby never got to complete the thought because Volant the eagle suddenly took center stage.

"OK, listen up everyone," said Volant loudly. "Today we are here to determine who deserves the title, *THE Fastest Flier in the Sky*! Will it be Swift ..." At this point the Free-tailed bats swarming over the peak roared in delight and encouragement! Quickly most of the Leaf noses and Pallids joined in, creating an incredible din.

"...or," Volant continued, "will it be Gabby?" The silence that followed was deafening, awkward, and embarrassing. As a judge to the event, Gabby didn't expect Volant to cheer for him. But why isn't Ollie the Osprey here to cheer? Gabby wondered.

"It's a simple point-to-point race," said Sully the Leaf-nosed bat leader, filling the uncomfortable void.

"Our competitors start here on the peak, then fly to the lighthouse at the marina over in town.

"First one to the lighthouse is the winner!" finished Flow the Free-tailed leader.

"Volant will depart now," said Sully, nodding to the eagle, "and go over and land on the lighthouse. Our eagle friend will be the judge if it's a photo finish."

"Good luck you two," said Volant, and with a flap of her enormous wings lifted off and departed, the bat swarm parting reverently as she passed through it.

Gabby suddenly felt even more nauseous, the only bird in the midst of thousands of bats. But there wasn't much time for squeamishness because once Volant made it most of the way to the town on the peninsula, Sully called the competitors to the starting line.

Chapter 34

"COMPETITORS ARE YOU ready?" Sully the Leaf-nosed bat, yelled. After a nod from both Gabby the seagull and Swift the Free tail, Sully continued, voice to the sky, "On your marks, get set, GO!"

Gabby flapped his wings to lift off, but not without noticing that Swift had simply dropped from her perch and was in flight, almost instantly. But then something unexpected happened: As Swift raced off the peak, she was immediately caught in the great cloud of bat admirers, all wanting to wish her well.

"Get out of my way!" Swift yelled. "You're in my path, MOVE!" But the bats still swarmed.

"Move everyone!" screamed Flow, Swift's Free-tailed compatriot, no longer pretending to be neutral now that the race had started.

Seeing the pileup, Gabby realized the advantage he'd been given and quickly rose above and away from it, knocking aside any bat that might get in his way. Gabby set his sights on the peninsula, pointed at the strobing lighthouse, and beat it away from the island with everything he had.

The bats continued to swarm around Swift, causing her to need to fly in the *opposite direction* of the peninsula just to free herself from the mob. By the time Swift broke away from her well-wishers and turned toward the peninsula, Gabby was just a dot far out over the water, the seagull's back lit up by the setting sun.

"Go with everything you've got," Swift thought to herself. And then aloud, Swift yelled, "Not so fast, Gabby, I'll catch you yet!"

And with that, Swift rocketed away. Some in the bat swarm followed, but the farther Swift went out over the water the more the following bat cloud thinned until at last it was just Swift.

Three-fourths the way across the water Gabby was beginning to feel confident. Looking back, he could see no sign of Swift. But the truth—a truth Gabby chose to ignore—was that darkness had fallen and Gabby couldn't see much of *anything* behind him, much less a small bat. So instead he focused ahead, on the lights of town and especially on the ever important, and ever enlarging, strobe of the marina's lighthouse.

When he could finally make out the outline of the lighthouse itself, illuminated by the marina lights, Gabby reckoned he was about a mile off shore. The seagull's confidence was growing by the minute and he silently urged himself on.

Suddenly Gabby sensed a presence next to him, and slowly turned his head to the right. It was Swift, who'd arrived out of nowhere, pumping those little wings in the strangest of fashion, yet showing no sign of wear. Gabby's beak dropped; he was flabbergasted.

"Well hello there Gabby Gab-ster," Swift said nonchalantly. "Miss me?"

Gabby had no chance to respond because in an instant Swift rocketed off!

Gabby pushed with all he had but in a few moments he realized that the race, for all intents and purposes, was over. Swift had caught him from far behind, and now quickly opened up a 10-meter lead, then 20, then 30.

Gabby lost sight of Swift in the dim twilight until they approached the breakwater edge of the marina. There city and marina lights threw a soft glow into the air. When Gabby next spotted Swift, the bat was 50 meters ahead.

Beyond Swift, the lighthouse was now clearly visible, and on top of it Gabby could see the dark outline of Volant the eagle waiting for them. Then Gabby saw Swift pass over the marina seawall. It would all be over in a matter of moments.

Chapter 35

BUT SUDDENLY A silhouette bolted out of the darkness, like a mini F-15, and smashed into Swift, knocking the bat out of the sky!

"What on Earth?!" yelled Gabby as he raced to make up the distance to where the mid-air collision occurred. "What just happened?!"

"*Ollie* just happened!" said a voice at Gabby's side. It was his quirky osprey friend who had appeared from above, out of nowhere.

"I told you I'd come and cheer you on, didn't I?" said Ollie with glee.

Gabby looked aghast. "But what did you do, Ollie?"

"What do you mean, what did I do?" said Ollie, clearly confused. "You want to win, don't you? We birds can't let those bats think they're faster than us. So I gave you a little help. Now you—and we birds!—can win the race! So GO!"

"But I don't want to win this way!" yelled Gabby back. "And what about Swift? Where's Swift?"

"Swift's in the water, floundering—look there!" It was a third voice, Volant the eagle's, coming alongside. "We need to help her!" Gabby quickly realized that Volant had seen all that occurred and had flown over from the lighthouse to join them.

"Oh...ah, hello Volant," said Ollie, voice changing from brash to respectful. "Um, what can I do to help?"

"Leave, Ollie," said Volant. "I think you've done enough already."

Looking first to Volant then to Gabby, Ollie's tone changed back again as he muttered, "Whatever. The silly bat will be OK. I could have eaten her, you know." With that, Ollie banked sharply and was gone.

Gabby bit his tongue, quickly turned away from the departing osprey, and returned to the issue at hand. "This isn't right, Volant. This was supposed to be a fair and square race. We've got to save Swift!"

Gabby dove for the water before Volant could respond. From above, the eagle could see the seagull splash land next to the broken bat.

"Swift, are you OK?" said Gabby.

"Barely," came the painful reply. "My wing really hurts—I think it might be cut. I can't swim, and I'm starting to sink!"

"Grab me," urged Gabby, paddling to come next to the flailing bat. Swift grabbed on but struggled to keep her head out of the water.

"OK, good Swift. Now you've *got to* climb on my back," said Gabby. "Then we'll figure something out after that. But first, we have to keep you from drowning! Come on Swift, climb—you can do it!"

Swift clawed her way inch-by-inch onto Gabby's back and then collapsed, unable to move further.

Gabby took his first deep breath since Ollie had so dramatically arrived. But just as he was letting his guard down, Volant swooped in yelling, "Gabby, there's a boat coming into the marina. MOVE or you two will get run over!"

Gabby looked up to see a boat rapidly approaching. He thought to fly but wasn't sure Swift could hold on even if he did get off the water. He tried to paddle but the boat was almost upon them. So in an act of desperation, Gabby flapped and squawked and flapped and squawked in his best goose-with-a-broken-wing impression.

All the chaos apparently worked. Just as it was about to run them down, the boat driver killed the motor and the boat slid to a halt right next to Gabby and Swift.

Chapter 36

GABBY THE SEAGULL stared up into the headlamps of five people, all of whom had come to the side of the boat. The boat teetered far off center, bringing them all that much closer as they peered over to inspect Gabby and Swift the Free-tailed bat.

"What, pray tell, do we have here?" said one of them at the front of the boat, a woman who wore an orange ball cap and had a short, tight ponytail.

"Hold it," said a younger woman, coming up beside her. The younger woman had a nose post and also wore a ball cap, though hers was blue and she wore it backwards. "Is that a bat on that seagull's back?!"

Even partially blinded by the headlamps, Gabby suspected what Volant, who'd landed back on the lighthouse, had already figured out. But any doubt Gabby had was removed when the dog stuck its head over the side of the boat and barked. It was the five people who'd been at the island several weeks back!

"Batey, be quiet!" said the man with the cycling cap, grabbing the dog's collar.

A second man, the one with heavy glasses, responding to the younger woman, said, "That is, indeed, a bat. A very soggy bat."

"Interesting," said the first woman, leaning farther out of the boat, now with a big flashlight in hand. "It looks like a Free tail, unlike most of the others we studied and captured today. Can somebody grab the net?"

"Wait a minute," chuckled the final person, an older fellow who was trying to line up a photo of the others through a big camera and lens. "Are you telling me we could have just stayed here in town to collect bats instead of exploring that new island and crawling around in caves since O-dark-30 this morning?!"

The other four laughed as the flash of the camera went off, blinding Gabby even further. The seagull shook his head—careful not to dislodge Swift— trying without success to clear his vision. But then, just as his eyesight began to return, Gabby felt himself caught up in a giant, rubberized fishing net.

"Careful, now," said the man with glasses to the younger woman as she brought the net alongside the boat. Then, with the net closer, he said, "Oh no, the bat looks injured, I think maybe its wing is torn."

The man with glasses exchanged a look with the woman with the orange ball cap. She pulled on leather gloves in a move that was direct and efficient.

"Tie Batey up in the back of the boat," she said to the man with the cycling cap.

"Done," he replied.

Once Batey was secure, the man with the glasses helped the younger woman lift the net, heavy with the perturbed seagull, into the boat. The woman with the orange ball cap slowly opened the net, intent on retrieving the nearly lifeless bat. "Quiet now," she whispered to the seagull, who was clearly agitated. When the woman reached into the net, the seagull squawked loudly and pecked at her hand.

"How strange," said the younger woman. "It's like the seagull is protecting the bat." The older man circled with his camera, recording each moment.

"It's OK," said the woman with the orange ball cap, ignoring them all and speaking to the seagull. "We will take care of your injured friend."

She gently lifted the bat from the bird's back, her hands protected by the leather gloves from the continuing assault of the seagull's hard bill.

"There you are, little injured Free tail," the woman said once she had extracted the bat. Looking closer, she said, "Oh gosh, it does indeed have a torn wing."

She held the bat out to the man with the glasses. As he took it from her, the woman continued, "We can add this one to the others we collected today, but it's going to need a bit of your veterinarian expertise."

The man with the glasses scrutinized the bat for some time, then looked up and in a matter-of-fact tone said, "Yes, that wing looks to be beat up pretty bad. But I can sew it back together. So agreed, let's add it to the others we collec..."

"No, please, let me take it," interrupted the younger woman with the blue ball cap. "Please? It just looks so scared," she added, a bit sheepishly.

The woman with the orange ball cap, the man with the heavy glasses, and the man with the cycling cap exchanged silent looks. After a moment, the woman gave a nearly imperceptible shrug, as did the man with the cycling cap.

"OK," the man with the heavy glasses said, voice softening. "That's probably a reasonable idea. This one needs special care or it's never going to fly again. Let's put it in that small box over there. Can you do that?"

"Yes, yes, of course," said the younger woman. "But just give me a second to find a soft cloth to put in the box to cushion its ride, OK?"

A few moments later the younger woman took the bat from the man with the glasses, lifted it gently into the air, and said, "I will look after you, little friend."

Chapter 37

FROM ATOP THE lighthouse, Volant the eagle watched with rapt attention. She saw the people in the boat gently rescue Swift the Free-tailed bat, then lower the net to the water and release Gabby the seagull.

Freed, Gabby squawked and squawked, scolding the people in the boat. Suddenly, Volant called out from above. The high-pitch, staccato scream drew Gabby's attention, momentarily quieting the seagull. Likewise, the five people in the boat looked up, surprised.

"Bald eagle, I think," said the older man, looking through his camera and trying to zoom in on the big bird. "Head looks white, though a little tough to tell in this low light. But then again, I thought they made a more awe-inspiring call."

"Does sound like a bald eagle to me," said the man with the cycling cap. "They make a short, piping sound just like that one's making. Funny, the movies often play a majestic screech when bald eagles fly across the screen, but that's actually the call of a red-tail hawk."

"Yes, agreed, bald eagle and just one more piece of a strange night," said the woman with the orange ball cap, turning back from looking at the big bird. Reaching for the key to the boat motor, she said, "Come on, let's get the bats we collected back to the lab and let them settle in. That, and taking care of our injured new friend here, and I think we can call it a day. We all need some rest. We've got a lot of work to do tomorrow."

The man with the glasses nodded his agreement. "Hard to argue with any of that. Along with packing everything up tomorrow, and now sewing up our new friend's wing, I have to wrap up the misting studies."

"I still don't think I understand what's going on with that misting work," said the older man with the camera.

"Pretty simple," returned the man with the glasses. "Vaccines, which will spur the bats to make antibodies, have the ability to prevent disease from taking hold in the host—in this case in the bat. Thus, a working vaccine can help stop disease transmission between bats, or disease spillover from bats to humans or other critters."

"That part I understand," said the man with the camera. "But why the mist?"

"Trouble is bats live in colonies, sometimes huge colonies," the man with the glasses continued, "and we could never inject enough of them with a vaccine to make a difference. But one possibility—a part of what I am testing—is that we could we spray the vaccine in a mist into a bat cave, or directly onto roosting bats, and get a substantial number of the bats to inhale it or perhaps lick it off their fur. Still, big questions loom. For example—and let's just assume we have a working vaccine for the disease we're targeting…"

"You mean like White-nose Syndrome?" the older man interrupted.

"…sure, like White-nose Syndrome. But also, like Hendra virus, or Ebola, or dozens of others—we can't forget that sometimes bats simply harbor the pathogens that cause the disease they pass along, including to humans, without themselves getting sick. But let's set that aside for a moment and go back to some key questions on misting. Even with a working vaccine, would a sufficient dose transfer from the mist into a bat's lungs when it breathes, and from there into its bloodstream, for the bat to gain immunity? Or likewise, if we were counting on the bats to lick the vaccine off their fur, could it pass through their digestive system intact to create immunity? And even if we knew one of those worked, could we really mist-vaccinate a high enough percentage of the bats in a huge colony to make a difference?"

"That helps a bit," said the older man with the camera looking, if anything, a bit more muddled. "How will you know if it works?"

"We're doing a tag, recapture study," said the man with the glasses. "I put an electronic tag under their skin. The next time we come back and locate the colony, we can scan for the tags. Once we find a tag, we can recapture each bat we misted. I'll take blood samples then and see if they've developed antibodies to the disease."

The older man smiled and then, thinking it easier to change topics, asked, "What about pulling the boat up? Do you want to do that tonight as long as we're here? Didn't you say you dry dock it at the lab between field seasons?"

"Yes, true," the woman in the orange ball cap, who'd been listening patiently, replied. "But we need it for one more run before we head home. Then we can pull it up for the season. Even if that weren't true, it's just plain time to call it a day."

"Or better, call it a *night*," yawned the man wearing the cycling cap.

Chapter 38

THE PEOPLE MOTORED slowly away. Unsure what to do next, Gabby the seagull took off and circled the marina squawking until the boat pulled up to the dock. Then Gabby flew up to join Volant the eagle on the lighthouse. Together the two birds watched as the five people unloaded the boat— coolers, nets, backpacks, and more, plus six cages— into the van.

The last item out of the boat was the small box holding Swift, one of the few items the people took into the van's passenger compartment. The younger woman with the blue ball cap on backwards held the box on her lap as the van door closed.

In another moment, the man with the glasses climbed into the driver's side and the van pulled away.

"They're taking Swift!" said Gabby in a panic. "We have to do something!"

"We *will* do something, Gabby, calm down," said Volant. "First, we need to find out where they're going and while you're panicking, they're getting away." Without another word, Volant launched off the lighthouse in pursuit of the departing van.

A moment later Gabby came alongside Volant, 60 meters off the ground, and the two birds followed the van away from the marina. Once beyond the edge of town all was dark, pierced only by the van's headlights. A mile or two on, the van turned into a lighted drive which ended at a recently constructed cinder-block building. The van parked along a side door to the building, and the five people got out and began to unload.

Volant nodded down to Gabby, then dropped silently to a fig tree close to the building. The big eagle landed on a solid upper branch there, hidden in the shadows, and watched the people work.

Gabby, meantime, could not see a flat enough spot on the fig tree to land, so instead he circled again. Finding nothing better, the seagull landed on a flat portion of the cinder-block building roof.

Gabby looked across at Volant with a shrug of the shoulders that seemed to say, "What do we do now?"

Volant made no response. Instead, she dropped her gaze and for the first time focused on the illuminated sign just below where Gabby stood. The sign read:

Instituto
de Enfermedades e Inmunología
Bio Safety Lab (BSL) 2

Chapter 39

LATER, AFTER THE people left, Volant the eagle watched as Gabby the seagull dropped inelegantly from the roof of the cinder-block building to a concrete wall alongside. Once there, Gabby hopped along the wall, bobbing his head side to side as he looked through the lab window for Swift the Free-tailed bat.

Gabby struggled to see by the light of the lone desk lamp still switched on. But then, suddenly, the seagull whooped, "Volant, I see Swift!"

The big eagle swooped down to join Gabby on the wall. "Where is she?" asked Volant as she landed.

"There, by the desk lamp," Gabby said. "But look—she's just lying listlessly there in that pitiful cage." Then the seagull yelled, "Swift, we're here! Swift, can you hear me? Can you see us?"

Gabby and Volant watched as Swift made a pained nod of her head, but nothing more. Looking further along the lab bench, Volant counted 12 more cages, each with a bat inside.

"Wait," said Volant, "I can also see Sonar and Starr ... and there are Pushy and Prickly, as well!"

"Great, that's just great," said Gabby, though with a flatter tone that showed his concern was for Swift, not the other bats.

Volant said nothing, letting Gabby's reaction slide, and instead paused in thought, surveying the scene. Finally, Volant looked up and said, "Look Gabby, the people are gone and nothing will happen for a while. Now that we're sure Swift is OK, I think we should fly back to the island and tell the bats what we've seen. They must be frantic to know what happened to Swift, and they'll be overjoyed to learn about the others being alive."

"I will not leave Swift!" said Gabby so strongly that it caused Volant to draw back.

Straightening, Volant said, "Look Gabby, we can't do anything here, at least not now. Remember how worn out the people were when they left. They said they wouldn't be back until lunchtime, so we have time to go to the island and still get back."

"You go," said Gabby unmoved. "I am staying! Swift is being held captive because of me, because of that stupid race that she won anyway, and because of that idiot osprey Ollie who was just looking after my ego. I am responsible. I will not abandon Swift!"

Chapter 40

VOLANT THE EAGLE crossed to the island as the sky was getting lighter, landing on the promontory just as the bats began to return from their night of hunting and collecting food. Most of the bats swept into the cave with only a short pause, but Sully the Leaf nose, Flow the Free tail, and Peevy the Pallid stopped immediately upon seeing Volant.

"What happened?!" said Sully.

"Yes, what?" repeated Flow. "Who won the race? Oh forget that—where's Swift?! She never joined us last night."

Volant took a deep breath, then told the story of how the race ended, how Swift was about to win, how Ollie the osprey dive-bombed Swift and knocked her out of the sky, how Gabby saved Swift only to have the people who had been at the bat cave capture her and take her away to a lab of some type, how...

"Wait! What?" shouted Flow. "The people have Swift?!"

"They do," said Volant. "Gabby and I looked in through the lab window and saw Swift in a cage, plus 12 more cages with bats in…"

"Did you see Sonar?!" shouted Sully.

"Yes," said Volant gently, "and Starr, Pushy, and Prickly, as well. They were in cages, too. It's been weeks, maybe a month since the people stole them away. But at least now we know they're still alive."

Chapter 41

THAT MORNING, AS Volant the eagle was filling in the bats on the island, Gabby the seagull remained on the concrete wall in front of the lab window. Gabby had planned to keep a constant overnight watch on Swift the Free-tailed bat. But all too soon after Volant's departure, Gabby had fallen asleep, worn from the excitement of the night.

With dawn, sunlight poured into the lab, throwing the seagull's shadow across the floor. Gabby came awake and quickly spotted Swift, thrilled to see that his injured competitor was now hanging, albeit stiffly and with one wing torn and folded at an odd angle, from a small branch in her cage. Gabby squawked and flapped and squawked and flapped until, most happily, Swift looked up through bleary eyes to see the ridiculous seagull making a spectacle in the window. Swift gave Gabby a downtrodden smile, causing the seagull to jump up and down even more.

"I am so sorry about what Ollie did to you," Gabby yelled. "That was not my idea and was not supposed to happen. You would have won, Swift."

Swift's pained smile grew a bit larger, signaling that while heavily filtered, sufficient sound was making it through the lab's ventilation system for the injured bat to hear.

"You are *The Fastest Flier in the Sky*," continued Gabby. "I know that now."

A sparkle came to the bat's eyes, giving Gabby great joy and for the first time hope that Swift would be OK.

"I will get you out of there, Swift!" said Gabby. "I promise you, my friend...and you *are* my friend. Volant and I will figure out a way."

Chapter 42

THE PEOPLE RETURNED to the lab around noon. Gabby the seagull continued his watch from the concrete wall, listening to their discussions through the vent and squawking wildly whenever one of the people came by the window.

"That's weird, isn't it?" said the man with the thick glasses to the woman with the orange ball cap. "I wonder if that could be the same seagull as last night."

"Stranger things have happened," returned the woman. "But no time to consider that, we need to get packed up today. Then tomorrow we need to release the bats back on the island they came from, get the boat settled, and make some miles heading north."

"Wait, we're not releasing all the bats!" It was the younger woman with the blue ball cap, which once again sat backwards on her head. "I'm taking the injured Free tail back to Montana for my research, remember?"

"What I remember," the woman with the orange ball cap, "is that I said we'd talk about it today. Why don't you start packing up the storage shed while I make a call." It was a flat statement, not a question.

As the younger woman walked away, looking at once deflated and hopeful, the man with the thick glasses gave the older woman a wry look.

"What are you gawking at?" she said.

"A *call*?" asked the man, with a knowing tone.

"I want to know what he thinks," the woman lamented. "He's had students all his life, and it's *his* granddaughter for goodness sakes."

The man shrugged his shoulders with a smile, then said, "And she's *our* daughter, and *your* intern for this work, and *you* are the project lead, lest you forget. Also, that bat is *not* going to heal without further care, and we don't have anyone to pass it on to here. Plus its swarm will be migrating soon. So if we leave it here the bat will d…"

Seeing the look the woman in the orange hat was giving him, the man with the thick glasses trailed off. Then he smiled, gave the woman a peck on the cheek, and headed for the door. "OK, I understand—call him and let's see what he says. In the meantime, I'll go help her pack up the shed."

Chapter 43

THE PROFESSOR, BACK in Oregon, sat in his favorite chair, absently reviewing a new textbook that one of his former students, now themselves a long-time professor, was readying for publication. Bored, the Professor looked up gratefully when his phone rang. He rose stiffly, found the phone in the kitchen, and answered. To his great delight, the Professor heard his daughter's voice on the other end of the line.

"How are you, dear?" he asked. "I was thinking about you a while back, with a question about a bat under the eave of the house. It had a...no, no, forget it, that can come later. How's your work in Baja going? And that husband of yours? And most important, how's my most wonderful granddaughter?"

"That's a lot of questions, Dad," the woman said, a smile apparent in her voice. "We got so much done in the field this time. Everything went great.... Well, maybe *great* isn't the right word. The detection dog we brought might have found the fungus that causes White-nose Syndrome."

"Ah no," said the Professor. "I recall many conversations we've had about White-nose Syndrome. Didn't you tell me it's killed almost seven million bats?"

"Yes," said the woman dolefully. "All since the disease arrived in North America around 2006. White-nose Syndrome may be the worst wildlife disease epidemic in North American history. It's in seven provinces and almost 40 states.

"That's truly alarming," said the Professor.

"Yes, truly alarming for our bat friends. I dare say *terrifying* wouldn't be too strong a word. Every day my colleagues and I worry White-nose Syndrome will turn up somewhere new."

The woman paused, but when she spoke again her voice turned playful. "By the way, though it's so sad, great memory to recall the 7 million deaths. Maybe *I*, for once, have taught *you* well!"

"Indeed you have," said the Professor. "I am always willing to be the student…as we all should be."

That made the woman smile as she continued. "We need to do the lab work, of course, to see if we can verify the fungus in the soil samples and skin swabs we took. Then we'll be able to tell if…"

"Back up a second," said the Professor, interrupting. "I thought White-nose Syndrome only occurs in colonies that hibernate during cold temperatures."

"Yes, that's true. That's what all the evidence tells us. But we also know that the Pd fungus that causes White-nose Syndrome can survive, at least for a time, at higher temperatures and on different surfaces." The woman's voice had gone deadly serious. "So could the fungus move with migrating bats from a hibernating colony to a non-hibernating colony and stay alive long enough to move on from there to another hibernating colony?"

"Seems like an important question to answer," said the Professor gently.

The Professor's calm words caused the woman to pause, smile, and take a breath. "Sorry, Dad, I know I'm getting worked up. We're just worried."

"Yes, I can hear that," said the Professor. "I can understand how the possibility that the dog detected the Pd fungus in Baja is cause for major concern."

"The local bats, especially the Leaf noses, we worked the most with on this trip don't hibernate, and I'm really not worried about them," continued the woman. "But there are others in Baja we also study that I am tremendously worried about.

"And those, I take it, hibernate?" the Professor asked.

"Maybe. There's a vesper bat, *Myotis peninsularis*, that lives only on the cape of Baja. To date we don't know what that species does in the winter, but they just might go into the Sierra de la Laguna..."

"The mountains in the center of the southern tip of Baja?" interrupted the Professor. "Am I recalling correctly?"

"Yes, exactly," said the woman. "And if they do winter at high elevations in those mountains, and hibernate, and the Pd fungus makes its way there, the entire species could be wiped out by White-nose Syndrome."

"What a terrible loss that would be," said the Professor. "Yet nothing surprises me much anymore. Seems like almost anything is possible." The Professor's voice had quieted as he talked, and the woman could almost see him taking off his glasses, as was his habit when deep in thought.

"A horrendous loss, Dad," said the woman, voice now trembling. "An entire species wiped out. Declining habitat, confined to a small geography— those bats are so vulnerable. That's why they're considered endangered. If White-nose Syndrome came to the Sierra de la Laguna, and *Myotis peninsularis* do hibernate there, they will be in deep trouble."

"That is a sobering thought," said the Professor.

"If White-nose Syndrome ever came to Baja, Dad," the woman said, "I would literally sit down on the beach and start sobbing. Like totally lose it sobbing. I'm tearing up just thinking about it."

Chapter 44

THE WOMAN IN the orange cap and her dad, the Professor, talked for a time more, until she realized she needed to bring the conversation to a close.

"Anyway, more on all that when we get back to Oregon," said the woman, her tone changing. "More on the entire trip, I promise, plus I want to hear what's going on with the aquarium."

"Yes, there is much to tell on that front," said the Professor.

"All in time," the woman continued. "We really need to get packing now, but before I go I have a different worry I want your opinion on."

"I'm all ears," said the Professor.

"Your granddaughter has really taken to one of our bats, one with an injured wing we've sewn back together," the woman said, her tone turning apprehensive. "That's where the big question comes in."

"Ah, my favorite kind," said the Professor, causing his daughter to laugh.

"Your granddaughter wants to take the bat back to Montana with her," the woman continued, "back to her lab as part of her thesis work. She wants to be responsible for seeing that bat heals, maybe even return it to the wild. I texted her major prof and she said it would take a bunch of paperwork added to their permit and likely some funds, but she could make it happen and is fine with the idea. So that's not an issue."

"Her major professor said *yes*, did she? What a surprise," said the Professor, the slightest lilt slipping into his voice.

"Yes, she did," said the woman, her tone flat. "Truth is, without further care the bat probably won't survive. But that aside, it's like your granddaughter has fallen in love with this little Free tail." Concern returned to the woman's voice, "I'm worried it's a school-girl's sentiment, not a scientist's, and I don't want to steer her the wrong way. You've had so many students over the years, Dad, what do you think?"

The phone went silent. After a long pause, the Professor said, "I think it's better to love science than to be afraid of it."

And that was it. Though she waited, the Professor said no more.

Finally, the woman sighed, then said, "Ok, message received. The bat goes to Montana. I love you, Dad. Now I gotta get back to packing. See you soon!"

Chapter 45

"TO MONTANA?" SAID Volant the eagle, newly returned, to Gabby the seagull. The two birds were perched atop the lab, watching for any movement.

"That's what the woman said. And they're only taking Swift!" exclaimed Gabby. "They said they're going to free the rest of the bats they captured."

"Great!" said Volant. "Yet curious. Why are they freeing all the bats, but not Swift?"

Volant's eyes grew distant for a few moments until Gabby interrupted the eagle's pondering, asking, "Have you ever been to Montana?"

"I have, indeed," said Volant, refocusing now on the seagull. Then, with a grimace, Volant added, "I was there one winter. Mostly along the Gallatin River. Brrr—what a cold, cold place it was to spend December and January! Haven't been back since. Sticking to the coast has been more my style. It's warmer."

"Well if they take Swift to Montana, that's where I'm going!" exclaimed Gabby. "I promised Swift I'd help her escape and that's what I am going to do. Will you go with me, Volant? Please...."

"Montana in the summer?" said Volant. "That sure has a better ring to it than *Montana in the winter*. Hmm... Yes, of course. Yes, we must help Swift. Yes, I'll go with you. But before that something else: Now that we know where Sonar, Starr, Pushy, and Prickly are, we need to make sure they're OK, too."

"Sonar and Starr, of course. But Pushy and Prickly?" said Gabby incredulously.

"Yes, even Pushy and Prickly," said Volant.

"OK," said Gabby, though with a voice that didn't sound convinced.

Chapter 46

VOLANT THE EAGLE and Gabby the seagull stood guard all afternoon while the people made ready to depart the next day. Volant perched atop the fig tree; Gabby atop the lab. Both watched as the people moved gear out of the main building and loaded it into the packing shed, or into a large truck and the trailer behind it.

Seeing no cages carried out of the building, Gabby regularly dropped to the concrete wall to look through the window and assure that Swift the Free-tailed bat was still in the lab. She was. Gabby also saw the people close down multiple computers, wipe down counters, mop floors, and lock cabinets.

The people worked fervently until long past dark, pausing only once when the younger woman in the backwards blue ball cap, who had earlier departed, returned with two bags of food and a six-pack of cold drinks. After a brief break to sit outside and eat, they all went back to work.

Late in the evening, the people climbed into their van and departed. Volant dropped down to the roof of the lab, where she knew Gabby could better land. A moment later, after taking a look to assure Swift was OK, Gabby flew up from the concrete wall to join Volant.

Gabby filled Volant in on all that had happened in the lab, finishing with, "And while most of them were moving stuff out and cleaning things up, the man with the glasses went to every one of the bat cages, lifted the bats out, and—not sure but I think—injected something under the skin of their backs, then stuck them with another needle..."

"Ouch!" said Volant.

"...and squirted their blood into a vial. Then the man would put each bat back in their cage, label the vial, write something in a notebook, and set the cage off to the side. While he was storing the vial in a cooler, one of the other people shuttled the cage he'd just set aside over to the door, making a big stack of them, as if getting ready to move the cages outside."

"Makes sense," said Volant. "They said they'd be letting the bats go tomorrow, right?"

"Yes, that's what they said," responded Gabby. "But there was one big problem: When the man finished with Swift he set her aside on another table. She's not at the door with the rest of them. Swift was by herself all day."

"Not with the rest, surely, because Swift's not being released," said Volant. "Being alone must have been tough on her when you're used to having so many friends around."

"I yelled encouragement and told Swift to stay strong and be hopeful," said Gabby. "But the man had moved her farther away from the window. I think she could still see me, but I don't think she heard anything I was shouting.

"How sad," said Volant, eyes troubled.

"Swift's only real contact all day," Gabby continued, "was when the younger woman in the blue ball cap came by to check on her. When the people left tonight the younger woman tried to take Swift with her, but the woman in the orange ball cap said, 'Absolutely not,' and made her put Swift back on the table."

Chapter 47

VOLANT THE EAGLE and Gabby the seagull spent an eventless night waiting and watching. Even though Gabby was too far away for Swift the Free-tailed bat to hear him well, the seagull still spent most of the night on the concrete wall. Gabby hoped that Swift might at least see his silhouette and know that he was there watching out for her.

At 2 AM, the glow of headlights turning in from the highway showed that the people had returned. They pulled the van up outside the door of the lab and four of them quickly formed a firemen's line to move the cages into the back of the van.

The fifth person, the old man with the camera, weaved in and out and around the group, shooting video and photos. Once Gabby heard him mutter to the man with the cycling cap, "I hope my shots come out in this low light. I really want a record of when we release them."

"It should be coming on sunrise by the time we get to the island and let the bats go," returned the man with the cycling cap. "I bet it'll be fine."

"True, I suppose," said the old man with the camera, though sounding unconvinced. "But at least here I have the outside lab lights to work with. The sun *better* be rising, or I'll probably mostly be shooting by headlamp."

When all the cages holding bats had been crammed into the van, the people loaded up, save two. The man with the cycling cap took Batey—along with a small rug, food, and water—to the shed. "We'll be back long before it gets hot," he said to the dog. Batey looked up unhappily, whining as the man locked the door.

Sensing the short pause, the younger woman with the blue ball cap said she needed a bathroom break before they left. She slipped into the lab, turned a light on, and checked on the lone bat still inside. The younger woman emerged only when the man with the thick glasses, sitting in the van's driver's seat, beeped the horn.

Chapter 48

VOLANT THE EAGLE followed the van back to the marina. Once there, she landed on the lighthouse, then watched as the people shuttled the bats to the boat, stacking the cages gently and securing them tightly.

As the people continued to make the boat ready for departure, Volant flew back to the lab and landed next to Gabby the seagull. Gabby continued to look in on Swift the Free-tailed bat and now, with the light on inside, it was apparent that Swift was looking back.

"Look Gabby," said Volant, "we can't do anything here. We know the people are headed to the island and we can beat them there. Rather than sitting here, we can be more useful if we catch Sully, Flow, and the rest on their way back into the cave this morning and tell them what's happening."

"But I can't leave Swift," said Gabby.

"I understand," said Volant. "But we know Swift is OK for now and we know when they return the people will take her to Montana. I'm sorry, but it's time to say goodbye—it's either now or a few hours from now."

Gabby took a long, sad look at his friend Swift. The seagull and the bat locked eyes, then Gabby gave a short wave, and yelled, "I will save you in Montana, Swift, I promise!"

Swift's eyes twinkled, as if she understood Gabby's message, even if the sound had not carried to her.

"And now, Gabby, come quick!" said Volant, lifting her wings to take flight. "We must get going to beat the people to the island! Can you imagine how excited the bats will be to know that most of their compatriots are going to be back by dawn?!"

Chapter 49

LATER, HAVING POSTED themselves on the promontory in front of the cave opening, Volant and Gabby waited patiently. Finally, as a hint of sunrise showed to the east, bats began to return to the cave.

Most of the bats bypassed the two birds, though some were upset, one complaining, "You two promised you'd get off the promontory when we enter and exit the cave. Come on, why are you in the way now?"

"Your friends that the people captured are coming back!" shouted Gabby in response. "They should be in the cave by sunrise! We came to tell you."

Soon enough word got around through the bat swarms—through the Leaf noses and Pallids and Free tails. As such, it wasn't long before bats swerving to avoid Volant and Gabby cheered the birds for the good news they brought.

AMONG THE LAST of the bats to arrive back to the cave from their night's hunt were Sully the Leaf-nosed leader, Flow the Free-tailed leader, and Peevy

the Pallid leader. All three had heard the good news
before they landed.

"Are they really letting Sonar go? And Starr?"
Sully asked in excitement.

"And Pushy and Prickly?!" cried Peevy, before
either bird had a chance to answer Sully.

"They *really* are letting them go," said Volant. "In
fact, the boat carrying them should be here any
minute."

After Sully and Peevy stopped beaming, an
awkward silence fell on the group. All eyes turned to
Flow. She, meanwhile, turned to face Gabby. "And
Swift, Gabby, will Swift be returned, as well?"

"I'm sorry," said Gabby. "But the younger
woman who was here is taking Swift back to
Montana when they depart."

"What! I don't believe you!" screamed Flow.

"It's true," said Volant. "But the good thing is
that Swift looks to be recovering and ...."

"But Free tails don't live in Montana," shouted
Flow, interrupting.

"... and Volant and I are going to follow them,"
said Gabby, cutting back in. "We're going to figure
out where they take Swift and how to set her free. I
give you my word."

"I don't want your word," said Flow. "What I
want is Swift safely back." Flow paused, grimacing

miserably. "But still, I can't go north with you. Our swarm needs to start back to Texas in a few d..."

Flow pulled up short, her words interrupted by the puttering of a motor. All eyes turned toward the water. Fifty meters offshore, they saw the running lights and dark outline of a motor boat rapidly approaching.

Chapter 50

"WE NEED TO release them from onshore," said the woman with the orange ball cap and short ponytail. She was talking to the older man carrying the camera as the man with the thick glasses steered the boat gently onto the beach.

The younger woman with the backwards blue ball cap hopped off the boat, splashing, and ran the bowline up to secure it to a post of the palapa. It was dark, but when the younger woman heard a noise, she lifted her headlamp to the palapa roof. An eerie set of yellow eyes shone in the beam of light, and the steep hill behind the palapa held the shadow of two large birds.

"That's a little spooky," the younger woman thought.

As the younger woman turned to walk back to the boat, she heard the older woman continuing with her explanation. "If we released them from the boat and one of the bats faltered on takeoff—it's been a while since they've flown—we'd have to rescue it from the sea. We've already done that once this trip, so we don't need to do it again."

Here the woman with the orange ball cap smiled at the younger woman with the blue ball cap. The younger woman paused long enough to roll her eyes and flash a knowing, if a bit pained, smile.

"Let's get going," said the man in thick glasses. "The bats are likely to be a bit disoriented when we let them go. We need them to get their wits about them before sunrise. And lest we forget, some of them are from other islands, though thankfully close by. It may take them a while to remember where their colony is and head to their roost for the day."

"Can you imagine the stories they could tell their friends?" said the older man with the camera.

Everyone chuckled, then set about moving the cages onto shore. The woman in the orange ball cap pointed to the younger woman in the blue ball cap when it came time to release the first bat. The younger woman pointed to herself, as if questioning, then smiled.

The younger woman donned leather gloves, took a breath, then opened the door of the cage that the man with the cycling cap held for her. She reached in gently, cooing softly, then slipped her hand around the bat inside.

Once she'd lifted the bat out of the cage, the younger woman turned slowly, lifted her hands high, then said, "Time to go home, little one" as she opened her hands.

The bat hesitated for a moment, as if unclear it was free to go, then it fluttered away. The people watched by headlamp as the bat circled them twice, before disappearing into the sky.

All the while, the older man with the camera had been positioning himself to record the moment. His photo caught the young scientist silhouetted on one side of the image, the dark outline of the island on the other side, just as the bat took flight into the orange sunrise glowing across the water.

Chapter 51

AFTER THE YOUNGER woman had released the first bat, everyone joined in to help, working rapidly. The man with the cycling cap helped move empty cages back to the boat; the man with the camera kept on filming. The other three, trained in handling bats, released bat after bat until in short order all 12 bats had been freed.

"Great effort, folks," said the woman in the orange cap. "I think every one of them made it!"

The older man and the younger woman high-fived, and soon the gesture passed through the group, accompanied by hoots of happiness.

"Time for coffee back in town," said the man in the cycling cap. "But first we need to get Batey out of the shed before it warms up."

"Amen to both of those," said the woman with the orange hat. "Then we can finish packing and get moving. It's a long drive back to Oregon."

"And we can't forget," said the man with the thick glasses, "that we need to stop in San Diego so *someone* and her special cargo can catch a flight to

Bozeman." He nodded to the younger woman in the blue ball cap, who smiled and did a mini-curtsy.

"Hey, let's also not forget you're dropping me!" chuckled the older man.

"Indeed, and with our gratitude," said the man with the thick glasses. "You've helped so much. Thank you for volunteering. It really matters."

"Yes, our great, great thanks to you!" said the woman in the orange hat.

The older man blushed as he looked between them, nodding his acceptance of their good words.

"I can't wait to see your photos from the bat caves," continued the man with the thick glasses. "One more critical piece of documentation on top of all the data we've collected."

"Yes, data, data, data—have we got data!" said the woman, causing the man in the thick glasses to smile. "Seems there's always too much data to analyze, yet somehow still never enough to be certain of anything!"

"Truer words could not be spoken," said the man with the cycling cap, having returned from untying the boat. "I think that uncertainty is why they call it *research*."

The woman in the orange ball cap smiled, while everyone else laughed, the mood decidedly light.

When the laughter quieted, the man with the glasses broke the silence, saying thoughtfully, "Or the uncertainty might come from a new approach, like Batey scenting fungus in the soil or scat. Is that really going to work? Seems impossible to believe he could detect the fungus. I can't wait to find out if it's true...."

The man in the cycling cap, still smiling, shook his head in mock disbelief as if to say, "We've been down this road a hundred times already." Then to no one's surprise, he said quietly, "*Always* trust the dog's nose!"

The smile on the woman in the orange ball cap dimmed, and she said, "I am worried half to death that Batey might have found the fungus, but even if he did we're better off finding it sooner rather than later."

"I'm equally worried," said the man with the thick glasses. And then, not wanting the happy mood to be lost, he looked to the woman in the orange cap and added, voice deadpan, "Hmm...you and me with the same opinion—maybe that's why we make such good partners." Everyone groaned while the man in the thick glasses bowed to the woman in the orange ball cap.

A smile came back to her face as the woman in the orange cap waved them off theatrically. "All right, all right, we will learn more once we get home and into the lab. But to *get* home we gotta *start* home. Let's go people. Everybody in the boat, it's time to point north."

As they moved to push off the boat, a loud squawk sounded near at hand. The people pulled up short in time see the outline of a seagull fly past, the bird chattering wildly. Before anyone could speak, another bird took flight from the palapa. This bird, far larger than the first, passed overhead as a dark apparition. The big bird made no sound, save the gentle whoosh from its massive wings.

Chapter 52

BY THE TIME the boat puttered into the distance, most of the bats circling the island had slipped into the cave. Only Sully the Leaf-nosed bat, Flow the Free tail, and Peevy the Pallid remained outside, waiting as Volant the eagle and Gabby the seagull returned to the promontory.

"Where are they?" demanded Sully and Peevy.

"The people released them a few minutes back," said Volant. "They'll be here soon."

"But no Swift?" asked Flow, disconcerted. "*Please* tell me they ended up bringing Swift, too!"

"I'm so sorry," said Gabby, "but..."

Suddenly, a mini-swarm of four bats interrupted Gabby, flying erratically and almost crashing into those assembled on the promontory. Sonar and Starr, the Leaf noses, and Pushy and Prickly, the Pallids, had returned!

Noisy chatter swept through the group as Sully and Peevy shouted their happiness over the return of their compatriots. A few late returning bats also dropped in to join the group on the promontory, adding to the din.

All the while Flow the Free-tailed leader stood aside, smiling weakly.

Eventually the cheering slowed and the bats turned from shouting their excitement and joy to peppering the returning refugees with questions.

"Where did they take you?"

"What was it like?"

"Did they feed you?"

"How many of there were you?"

"Were all the bats just from our island?

"Other islands?"

"Close by or far away?"

"Any of our fish-eating friends?"

"Why did you crash-land into us?"

"Did you forget how to fly?"

Chapter 53

"SLOW DOWN, SLOW down," said Volant the eagle, stepping forward to break up the chaos.

"Yes," said Sully the Leaf-nosed leader. "Slow down! We are all excited, but let's let them breathe. So much to tell, and I'm sure we will learn it all eventually. But sun's coming up so we bats need to get into the cave pretty soon."

"But not yet!" exclaimed Flow the Free-tailed leader. "Before we do anything the most important question is *where is Swift?*"

Sonar and Starr, the Leaf noses, looked between themselves, smiles fading. Then Sonar drew himself up and said quietly, "Swift is still at the lab."

Flow deflated.

"They said they were taking her to Montana," Starr added miserably.

Flow turned to Gabby with a look of deep sadness, showing her acceptance now that what the seagull had told her was true.

Gabby lowered his eyes, but said nothing.

"Whatever," said Peevy the Pallid bat leader, dismissing the discussion. "What I want to know NOW is did they hurt you?! If they did I'll…"

"No, not really," said Pushy. "Mostly it wasn't that bad."

"What do you mean *wasn't that bad*, you moron?" It was Prickly, the other Pallid bat and Pushy's irritable companion. Pushy, who usually took guff from no one, cringed and melted into the background.

"They kept us in tiny cages with nothing more than a single branch to hang from!" Prickly continued. "They stuck needles in us, and injected something under the skin of our backs.

"What?" shouted the gathered bats in unison, Peevy's voice ringing out the loudest.

"And that's not even the worst of it," continued Prickly, obviously enjoying her notoriety. "They sprayed us with a mist."

"No!" the bats shouted. Most of them hated getting wet.

"Yes, a mist that stunk," Prickly continued. "They said it was an experiment that they'd already shown could stop a disease that kills bats. WHAT A JOKE! Their miracle mist itself made a bunch of bats sick …."

"How many got sick? Did Swift get sick?" It was Flow jumping in.

"Swift was fine," admitted Prickly.

"And the other bats?" Flow asked.

"I suppose most of them...OK, all of them...were fine. No one got sick, but they could have," said Prickly with a sneer in her voice.

"So then, help me understand," said Volant, "like the rest of the bats you two didn't get sick from the treatment?"

"Yes, we did not get sick. But no, we were *not* like the rest!" scoffed Pushy, who had stepped forward again, re-energized by Prickly's nod. "We were smarter! Unlike the others, we escaped the misting. The branches in our cages had big leaves on them. We wrapped ourselves in the leaves so we avoided whatever it was they were trying to poison us with."

"Wait," said Volant, eyes registering confusion. "They said the mist would stop you from getting a disease that could kill you, no one else got sick, and you rejected it?"

"Darn right," sneered Prickly distastefully. "We Pallids eat scorpions. Most of us have been bitten— do you think we're scared of a little disease?"

Before Volant could respond, Peevy pushed herself back into the discussion, saying, "And as every Pallid knows, scorpion venom cures any disease!"

"We will *never* get sick!" shouted Pushy.

"Absolute truth," concluded Prickly. "Stupid mist. I cannot believe that the rest of those idiot bats just sat there and took it!"

Chapter 54

AFTER THE BATS headed into the cave, it didn't take long for Gabby the seagull to make his plans known to his friend Volant the eagle. They sat alone on the promontory watching the day find itself.

"We need to go now," Gabby said. "We need to head north to Montana."

"Now?" said Volant. "I know how bad you want to go, but there's something I've been wondering about: I thought you western gulls didn't like going inland so much?"

"Yes now!" exclaimed Gabby. "As for getting away from the sea, I'll get over it—that doesn't matter. What matters is that the people have already left with Swift!"

"But hold on one more time. We heard them: the younger woman is taking Swift to Montana on a jet. Even if you were *The Fastest Flier in the Sky*, there's no way we could keep up with a jet."

Gabby's look turned sour. "Guess I hadn't thought of that," the seagull said.

"Don't look so glum," Volant continued. "I've been to Bozeman, the town where they're taking

Swift. And we know what the young woman looks like that is holding our friend. We will get to Montana, it will just take us some time. And when we do, we will rescue Swift."

"Do you really think so?" said Gabby.

"I really do," said Volant.

"OK, but we still need to get going soon," said Gabby. "Winter is done and even if it's still a little chilly as we head north, we can't dally."

"Ah, sadly, I suppose that's true," said Volant, her voice uncharacteristically dispirited. "I thought we'd have another month of this glorious spring weather here in Baja. And it's so beautiful, just look out there..."

Here Volant tilted her head out to the east, sun still low to the horizon, sea shimmering.

"Beautiful," Gabby agreed.

"Hey wait!" said Volant, suddenly focusing. "A whale just rolled out there near the other island. Did you see it?"

"No," sad Gabby. "I can see a couple of dolphins jumping halfway to the island, but no whale."

"Ah, no, you missed it. The whale is off the point," said Volant. "We need to check if it's Spouts and Jessie. And by *we* I mean *you* have got to fly out there."

"Really?" said Gabby, even though knowing he was always the best choice for such a mission. Unlike

Volant, he could land on the water to check if their friends, the gray whale and turtle, had finally arrived in Baja from back in Oregon.

"I want to find them as much as you," Gabby said. "But I must have dropped in on a hundred whales since we've been down here, and not one of them has been Spouts. And none of them have even heard of a turtle named Jessie."

Volant gave Gabby a silent look that carried a clear message: "We need answers, not excuses."

"But maybe they didn't make it down to Baja," tried Gabby. "Or maybe Spouts dropped Jessie off somewhere and is already headed back to Oregon."

Volant remained silent, though her piercing gaze intensified.

"OK, OK," Gabby muttered. "I'm going, I'm going." And with that, the seagull took off from the promontory, head shaking from side to side.

Chapter 55

GABBY THE SEAGULL flew out toward the end of the neighboring island, then began to circle and watch the water's surface. Gabby was certain he'd spot the whale the next time it blew, but held little hope he'd discover Spouts the gray whale and Jessie the turtle.

But Gabby was in for a surprise!

When the whale next came topside and blew its column of salty mist, Gabby dropped out of the sky. The closer he came to the whale the more excited Gabby got. "Wait, that *does* look like Spouts!" he thought.

Gabby bee-lined it for the whale, catching it just as it was starting to dive again. Now Gabby was certain and screamed, "Spouts, it's me, Gabby, from up north!"

The whale stopped its dive, looking up in surprise as the seagull landed on his back.

"Gabby?" shouted Spouts. "Gabby!" The whale was so excited he gave a massive celebratory splash of his tail resulting in a wave that threw Gabby into the air.

Laughing, Gabby splashed down into the water in front of Spouts and they bobbed along on the waves together.

"How are you?" asked Gabby.

"How are *you*?" responded Spouts, answering a question with a question, and then another one: "What have you been doing here, anyway? Is Volant around?"

TWENTY MINUTES PASSED where Spouts wouldn't answer a question—not about Jessie the turtle or their trip south—so intent was the whale on learning what Gabby and Volant had been doing since they all were last together on the Oregon Coast.

"…and so," Gabby said, winding down, "because Swift, our Free-tailed bat friend, is on her way to Montana, that's where we're heading next, maybe even starting tomorrow."

"Montana? Hmm…," said Spouts. "Don't think I'll be seeing you there."

"No, that's probably a safe bet," chuckled Gabby. "But I'm sure we'll see you back in Oregon one day soon. But please, enough about us! How did your trip south go? More importantly, where is Jessie?!"

"Jessie didn't make it to Baja," Spouts said.

"Oh no," said Gabby in alarm. "What happened?"

"No, no, nothing bad," said Spouts. "But she got an offer she couldn't refuse."

"What do you mean?" asked Gabby.

"Remember the pod of white-sided dolphins that left Oregon with us?" continued Spouts. Gabby nodded and Spouts continued, "They were headed to Baja, as well. We had an eventful trip down the coast, the lot of us, all becoming pretty tight. When I dove and couldn't look after Jessie, the dolphin pod kept her safe."

"That was good of them," said Gabby. "But still, where's Jessie now?"

"Probably halfway across the Pacific," said Spouts in a matter of fact voice.

"What?!" said Gabby, not sharing Spouts nonchalance about a swim across the ocean.

"Jessie was always cold, remember?" said Spouts.

"Of course," said Gabby. "That's why Volant and I asked you to take her south."

"Yes, yes," said Spouts. "Anyway, as we came down the coast we crossed path with a couple of leatherback turtles. That was quite a moment! We all circled around as Jessie told the two leatherbacks her story. When Jessie finished, the older of the two turtles, who had been nodding knowingly, said, 'Sounds to me, Jessie, like you don't even know who you are. Let me clear it up for you: You, my new friend, are a leatherback turtle, just like us.'"

Gabby gasped!

"There's more," said Spouts. "The old leatherback told Jessie that the reason she was cold is she must have been captured in warm waters. Then the younger of the two turtles explained, 'Some leatherbacks live in warm waters, some in cold waters.'

"The older turtle continued, 'The waters of Australia are warm, and that's where we're headed. It'll be my last crossing of the Pacific Ocean. Why don't you join us?'"

"OK, now I get it," Gabby said, the light bulb coming on.

"Jessie looked to me, then looked at our new dolphin friends," Spouts said. "Every one of us told her she should go. After a pause, Jessie shouted, 'YES!' And so part way down here to Baja, Jessie took a hard right with a couple of her own kind, leatherback turtles. The three of them straight-lined it for Hawaii, their first stop on the way to Queensland, Australia!"

Chapter 56

WHEN SPOUTS THE gray whale finally lifted his tail and dove, Gabby the seagull raced back to the promontory. With great excitement, he filled Volant the eagle in on all he'd learned from Spouts about Jessie the turtle, the dolphin pod, and the two leatherback turtles they'd met.

"So Jessie is on her way to Australia, with two new turtle friends to look after her?" said Volant, as Gabby's story came to a close. "Good for her! I've always wanted to go to Australia. Just think of it: kangaroos and koala bears, wallabies and wombats!"

"Cool enough," returned Gabby. "But I've always wanted to see a platypus. Sort of a beaver with a duckbill?! How can that possibly be?"

"Nothing surprises me much anymore," said Volant. "Seems like almost anything is possible."

Chapter 57

THAT DAY VOLANT the eagle and Gabby the seagull made their decision: It would be their last day at the island. The next day they would start flying north.

At sunset, the two birds sat near the top of the promontory, watching and waiting. The western sky turned a deep orange. Soon bats began to emerge from the cave in a pattern they'd long grown used to: first in a trickle; then twenty at a time, then fifty, then by the hundreds. Soon thousands of Leaf-nosed, Free-tailed, and Pallid bats flitted by them on the start of their nightly search for food.

At last Sully the Leaf-nosed leader and Flow the Free-tailed leader appeared. The bats saw the two birds, zipped in a loop and returned, then settled on the big cardón cactus. As the two birds hopped over to join them, Sonar the Leaf-nosed bat, and Peevy, Pushy, and Prickly, the Pallid bats, dropped in, as well.

"Gabby and I have something to tell you," said Volant. "We're heading north tomorrow."

"I kind of figured that would be coming," said Sully.

"But not to Oregon, right?" said Flow, almost pleading. "You are going to Montana, right? You gave me your word that you'd rescue Swift."

"Yes!" responded Gabby. "Volant and I *are* going to Montana to rescue Swift. I promise."

"I am holding you to it," said Flow solemnly. "It's the only thing that allows me to start our colony heading back to Texas. And I've decided, too—we depart tonight."

"What?" asked Starr the Leaf-nosed bat, having just arrived during Flow's last words. "Did I hear that right, the Free tails are leaving tonight?"

"Yes, they are," responded Sully. "And our two bird fr...."

"And so are Pushy and Prickly," said Peevy, butting in.

"You two are leaving, too?" said Volant, turning to the two Pallid bats.

"But you live here," said Sonar.

"Pallids can migrate, too," said Pushy.

"We need some new scenery, maybe even see what living in cooler temperatures is like," said Prickly.

"We may even try hibernating," said Pushy, mocking a yawn.

"We want to go to a place where no one bothers us," Prickly continued. "We're thinking California."

Gabby winced.

"But what about the bats there?" asked Volant. "How do you know they'll welcome you?"

"Of course they'll welcome us!" scoffed Prickly. "Why wouldn't they? We're Pallids, after all."

Chapter 58

IT WAS 30 minutes later. Volant the eagle and Gabby the seagull remained on the promontory. All the Leaf-nosed and Pallid bats had left to hunt, except Sully and Starr, the Leaf noses, who were still hanging on the cardón cactus.

Flow the Free-tailed leader also remained, though she had just directed her swarm to get started toward Texas. "It's time," said Flow with sadness in her voice. "I've got to go and catch my group."

"Good bye, Flow," said Starr.

"Good bye, dear friend," said Sully.

"May we see you again next year," returned Flow.

"And may you once again have Swift with you," said Volant.

Flow looked briefly at Volant, sighed, then turned to stare directly at Gabby. Gabby nodded earnestly, and was extending a wing to wave just as Flow turned and took flight.

Chapter 59

AS THE FREE-TAILED bat swarm receded into the distance, Volant the eagle turned back to face Gabby the seagull. Sully and Starr, the Leaf noses, were the only bats still on the promontory.

"Gabby, I know we said we'd depart tomorrow," said Volant, "but maybe we should go now. We can say goodbye to Sully and Starr before they take off for the night. What do you think?"

"I've been ready for days," said Gabby. "Plus I like the idea—a night flight might be a fun way to get going."

"Night flying is the best," said Sully.

They all laughed. It was a moment of happiness but as the laughter subsided, an awkward silence fell.

"I'm not good with goodbyes," said Sully finally. "So Starr, I think it best we just bid our friends adieu and join the rest of our swarm."

"Good bye, friends," said Sully. Starr looked to be crying.

"Good bye, friends," returned Volant and Gabby in tandem, though before their words were out the bats had already rocketed away.

Chapter 60

VOLANT THE EAGLE and Gabby the seagull looked around, suddenly alone on the promontory. Sunset had passed but the western horizon still glowed with yellows and oranges. To the east, stars began to emerge, first by tens, then hundreds, then thousands. The sea was magically calm, its surface twinkling on and off, mirroring the stars.

Below them, a lone sea lion cruised the shore. Volant and Gabby hadn't seen a sea lion on this side of the island since that first night they'd arrived. As with that night, a thousand twinkling lights traced the sea lion's path through the sea.

"I love this place," said Volant wistfully, looking at the scene below.

"I do, too," said Gabby. "But it's time we depart."

"I suppose it is," said Volant, straightening up, giving a little shake, and looking for the North Star. Lifting her wings, Volant said, "Off we go, my friend."

Volant and Gabby took flight from the promontory. Though their path had been unstated, they both pointed for the town on the peninsula. Once there, they looked down on the marina and spotted the lighthouse. Then they followed a dark road up the coast until they came to the lab where Swift and the others had been held.

Twice they circled the lab, enjoying the cool breeze. Both thought about Swift and about Montana, but soon enough the anticipation of taking a long, long flight took precedence, filling them with happiness.

Volant slipped out of their circling pattern first, and pointed north, a mild tailwind pushing her forward. Gabby soon came abreast. For a time the two friends basked in the delight of flight, of riding the gentle air currents, of the cool breeze slipping across their faces and over their wings, of the sense that they could go on like this forever.

It was the purest joy either of them ever felt. Soon Gabby looked over to Volant, a smile on his face, certain his eagle friend was as enchanted in that moment as he.

Volant smiled back knowingly, then said, "Alright, Gabby, my friend and, for the record, *The Second Fastest Flier in the Sky*, it's time for us to head to Montana."

Epilogue

EARLY ONE MORNING, three months later, Volant the eagle and Gabby the seagull spiraled upward into the wakening day, the sun just peeking over a ridge to the east. Each revolution brought the two friends higher along the front of Montana's Bridger Range. Soon they climbed into the cold sunlight, though below on the hillside the large, white "M" remained in the shadows.

Once in the sun, Volant and Gabby turned south. From the edge of the mountains, they flew over a bustling city until they came to a peaceful college campus. In the center of campus was a stately brick building, a magnificent white tepee on one side, the statue of an exceptionally large bobcat on the other.

Volant and Gabby flew on, knowing their goal was further along, on the far edge of campus. Soon they flew over a low-lying building, with a sign along the front walkway that read:

MSU Wildlife Disease Lab (BSL-3)

Passing over the building, they circled in on a pasture adjacent to it. The pasture was empty save a water tank and trough, a tree, and a single, very large animal. Volant landed on a bare lower branch of the tree, Gabby on the water tank. Spotting the birds, the large animal, a bison, trotted across the pasture from the lab window it had been gazing into.

"Volant, Gabby, good to see you two again!" said the bison.

"And you, Ralphie," said Volant. "Good to see you again, as well."

"Yes, yes, yes, all that's great," said Gabby. "I'm sure we are all happy to see each other again. But that's not why we're here. This time, Ralphie, you must show us where Swift is!"

"As I promised, I will do that," said Ralphie, a bit taken aback by Gabby's abruptness. "And today I can. But first there is something I...."

BUT LET'S STOP here. It turns out the stories of how Volant and Gabby met Ralphie the bison, how Ralphie met Swift the Free-tailed bat, and how both the bison and the bat sought their freedom, as well as the story of Jessie the turtle's crossing of the Pacific Ocean to the intriguing world of Australia, are themselves captivating tales best left for another day.

Afterword

As mentioned in the Author's Note at the front of the book, I think it is important to let you the readers know that much science is incorporated into BAT CAVE: A FABLE OF EPIDEMIC PROPORTIONS. That science is presented intermittently throughout the story, sometimes gently, other times more overtly, just as it was in FISH TANK: A FABLE FOR OUR TIMES. Briefly, allow me to provide a few important concepts and caveats underpinning BAT CAVE:

- Bats, of which there are over 1400 species, make up ~20% of all mammals worldwide. They are important to ecosystems (and mankind), performing such critical ecological services as eating insects and pollinating plants.

- Bats can harbor pathogens[3] that can cause myriad forms of disease, in many cases without

---

[3] For those who wish to be a bit wonky, bat and disease experts note that unless that microorganism (e.g., virus, bacteria, fungus) causes disease in the host, it isn't a "pathogen." Since many of the microorganisms that bats carry do not

the bats themselves being sick. They can pass along some diseases to people or other animals, a process called "spillover," or to other bats.

- The virus that causes COVID has moved from people to wild animals, including deer (though not to our knowledge, thus far, to bats). In these animals, the virus will be under different selective pressures and might mutate into a new version not covered by vaccines designed for a previous "variant." If the new variant is passed back to humans, another human COVID disease cycle might result, possibly with worse sickness than the original. Thus, in part, the keen interest of the scientists in BAT CAVE for learning the COVID infection status of the bats.

- White-nose Syndrome (often "WNS") has caused greater than 90% declines in three species of hibernating bats in North America. As of this writing, WNS is known to be in 39 states and seven provinces.

---

cause disease *in bats*, those microorganisms should not technically be called "pathogens." In such cases, it would be more correct to say that the bat is harboring a microorganism that if transmitted into another host can become a "pathogen" (i.e., cause disease). In the story of BAT CAVE, the Pd fungus can cause disease (WNS) in at least some species of bats, so in those bats calling Pd a "pathogen" is warranted. Ugh, I know—semantics, right? As with life, science and science communication are rarely black and white, but instead include much nuance. Thankfully, stories of eagles and seagulls and bats can provide a softer path for introducing and working our way through such intricacies.

- White-nose Syndrome is known to be caused by a fungus, the "Pd"—short for *Pseudogymnoascus destructans*—fungus. Bats can test positive for the fungus before actually having WNS disease.

- Twelve bat species in North America are known to have WNS. Six bat species are known to have the Pd fungus but not WNS.

- The Pd fungus that causes WNS can be spread by bat-to-bat contact. Since most bats who develop WNS die, stopping the spread of the Pd fungus is paramount if bats are to be saved.

- Bats of different species sometimes roost together, meaning WNS can move not only between bats of a single species, but also from one bat species to another.

- Bats migrate, often great distances, giving any microorganisms, pathogens, or diseases the bats may carry the opportunity to spread widely (though many other factors are at play, as well).

- While there may be birds faster than a seagull, having Swift race for title of *The Fastest Flier in the Sky* is warranted. Mexican free-tailed bats can fly up to 100 miles/hour and are touted as the fastest animal, traveling horizontally, in the world.

- Pallid bats range widely, from western Canada to the southwestern USA, the Baja Peninsula, and central Mexico. While Pallid bats are found in California, they are not known to migrate between California and Baja. Still, depending on location, some Pallid bats do hibernate—as Pushy suggests they might try in California—considered a necessary function for WNS to take hold. BAT CAVE leaves readers unsure if, but suspecting that, Pushy and Prickly may possibly have been exposed to the Pd fungus that causes WNS. Thus, the two bats' plan to migrate to California provides readers an important symbol of the reality noted above: Many bat species migrate and can carry microorganisms, pathogens, or disease with them to new areas, thus exposing other bats (and other creatures) to disease spread.

- Mist vaccination, with potential methods and limits as described in BAT CAVE, is among the (largely) experimental possibilities for helping bats survive WNS and other diseases. Misting techniques may be done with a classic vaccination approach that targets increasing the immunity of—and, hence, survival rates of—bats exposed to the Pd fungus and thus at risk of developing WNS.

- All scientific evidence to date indicates that hibernation is required for White-nose Syndrome to manifest. Bats have to be cold and in torpor (i.e., lowered physiological activity, as in hibernation) for the Pd fungus to grow and invade their skin tissues. The Pd fungus that causes WNS has been found in warmer climates. Given bat migration, it is possible that the Pd fungus could move from a cold location where bats hibernate, to a warmer location where they don't, and then on to another colder location.

- Dogs have incredible noses—thousands of times more sensitive than humans—that are being employed to achieve important conservation and health goals. Dogs can, for example, use their sense of smell to find invasive plants, insects, and fish, as well as endangered or threatened species. Dogs can also find disease. For example, they can detect metabolic changes caused by cancer or COVID on the breath of people or the sweat of individuals. As of this writing, to the author's knowledge dogs are not used to detect White-nose Syndrome, or the PD fungus that causes WNS. That dogs could be used in such efforts, as described as an experimental effort in BAT

CAVE, is within the realm of possibility, though many issues would need to be addressed, including that of animal safety (e.g., dogs themselves contracting a disease from bats).

- Scientists doing research in the field employ best practices for protecting the animals they are studying, including bats. Removing bats from the field to a laboratory setting, as described in BAT CAVE, would not be typical for most studies. It is not necessary, for example, to take bats into a laboratory setting to sample for the Pd virus, although it might be done for the imagined mist vaccination studies described in BAT CAVE. Ethical experimental plans for animal research generally follow guidelines described by the Institute of Animal Care and Use Committees. Those guidelines include goals such as minimizing handling time and animal stress.

- While possible, it would not be typical for scientists to take a bat home to their research institution, or to transfer a bat across an international boundary.

- Tackling many (most?) big science questions requires a collaborative approach. Shared knowledge from across disciplines (in BAT CAVE the research team had expertise in at least ecology, immunology, epidemiology, veterinary science, bat behavior, and dog detection) is of critical importance, as is the inclusion of traditional ecological knowledge, senior and junior scientists, and volunteers.

- A small cadre of talented, dedicated scientists are seeking to unravel the mysteries found at the intersection of bats and disease. The dedication of those scientists to, and importance of, their work is a beautiful story in and of itself.

- Young scientists and citizen scientists can and do have impact. To do so requires, to the mind of this author, four key requirements. The first three are curiosity, a hunger for learning, and a willingness to step into the unknown. The fourth is finding a mentor willing to share their expertise, guidance, and connections—be those in the field, the lab, or the sphere of ideas—and, most importantly, willing to share their time.

Bat species highlighted in BAT CAVE

California leaf-nosed bat *
(*Macrotus californicus*)
Sully, Sonar, Starr

Insectivore; uses eyes and echolocation
(photo: National Wildlife Service, public domain)

Pallid bat
(*Antrozous pallidus*)
Peevy, Pushy, Prickly

Insectivore and arachnivore (eats scorpions!);
also eats *cardón* cactus; uses echolocation and hearing
(photo: Connor Long)

Lesser long-nosed bat *
(*Leptonycteris yerbabuenae*)
Lepto, Luna

Primarily eats nectar from night-blooming cacti; also fruit and pollen
(photo: Cecil Schwalbe, National Park Service, public domain)

Mexican free-tailed bat
(*Tadarida brasiliensis*)
Flow, Swift

Insectivore; uses echolocation; some migrate from the USA to Baja
(photo: Ann Froschauer, US Fish & Wildlife Service, public domain)

Fish-eating bat
(*Myotis vevesi*)
Lives on adjacent island

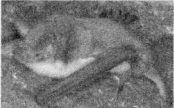

Eats mostly fish and crustaceans; have large feet and sharp claws
(photo: CC4.0 International, https://journals.plos.org/plosone/artic le?id=10.1371/journal.pone.0025845)

A vesper bat
(*Myotis peninsularis*)
Bat species described as living only on the southern tip of Baja

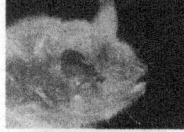

Insectivore; endangered; threats include tourists and disease
(photo: Juan Cruzado Cortés, under CC4.0 International)

Little brown bat
(*Myotis lucifugus*)
In the Professor's cave and at the Redwoods

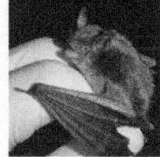

Insectivore; primarily uses echolocation to find prey
(photo: S M Bishop, under CC3.0)

---

* Note that long-nosed bats are also leaf-nosed bats. Both belong to the family Phyllostomidae, which all have nose leafs.

In Gratitude

MANY EARLY READERS had an impact on BAT
CAVE: A FABLE OF EPIDEMIC PROPORTIONS, and hence
on my vision for the book, and I would like to
express my great appreciation to them. The book's
shortcomings are mine; its strengths emanate from
the collective community of colleagues and
researchers, friends and family, who set aside their
valuable time to help me, be their efforts focused on
story, science, or both.

First and foremost, I want to thank Dr. Winifred
Frick, Chief Scientist at Bat Conservation
International and Adjunct Professor of Ecology and
Evolutionary Biology at University of California
Santa Cruz. I got lucky when I first wrote "Fred" to
ask if she might be willing to be a once-through
reader for BAT CAVE. I think Fred may have been
intrigued by the idea of someone writing a story that
started in Oregon, where she got her PhD at Oregon
State University, then transitioned to a bat cave in
Baja, where she has done much field research. When
I added that the book would be highlighting the
danger of White-nose Syndrome, a crisis to bats and

a focus of Bat Conservation International, I think Fred was hooked. She not only read the book, making strong and pointed comments on my scientific inaccuracies (though always being diplomatic!), she helped me further hone science aspects of the story through extended email dialogues. Many times we discussed the tradeoff between story and truth as supported by science, and balancing such truth with what might be unknown yet at least possible for the plotline. For me those discussions were a profound honor because time, a precious commodity for us all, is even more so for a world-leading expert in their field like Dr. Frick. I am greatly indebted to Fred for her kindness, help, and expertise. While many scientists helped fact check me along the way (thank you all!), it is in large part because of Fred that key science aspects of BAT CAVE are solid. Any faults in the book related to bat science (or beyond) are mine, be they inadvertent or small side steps I made in the service of story.

Bat Conservation International (BCI) deserves special note. The group seeks to conserve the world's bats and their ecosystems to ensure a healthy planet. BCI is dedicated to stopping the extinction of bat species. Key goals driving BCI include being passionate, collaborative, and science-based in their work (concepts I sought to capture in BAT CAVE). I commend BCI to your review and support—a good starting place is at *https://www.batcon.org/*.

Thanks also to Dr. Raina Plowright—past of Montana State University, now of Cornell University—who first opened my eyes to the wonder of bats and disease. A few years back, Raina was kind enough to allow me to help her write a major grant on the study of disease spillover. Raina, herself a world-leading expert in her field of epidemiology, answered myriad texts regarding bats and disease. She answered them quickly, and because she was overseas on sabbatical, sometimes in the middle of her night! Not surprisingly, it was Raina who introduced me to Fred, acknowledged above.

I want to thank artist Katie Lindberg for allowing me to include her incredible paintings and drawings as part of BAT CAVE. Katie has the unique ability to make other's imaginings come to life on paper, of visualizing a story and bringing it to us all in her own unique and wonderful way! I so appreciate Katie's patience and skills in dealing with my meandering requests. I so appreciate Katie's artistic talents.

I appreciate the guidance and insights and hard questions—be they about story or science or critters or Baja—from my "best-est" editor friend ever, ecologist Linda Ashkenas at Oregon State University. Linda has been a positive force for almost every book I've written.

I appreciate the insights from two authors, Eva Silverfine Ott and Tom Vandel, both of whom helped shape the story that resulted here after kindly reading an early version of BAT CAVE. Both Eva and Tom have outstanding writing talents and cover topics that make their books deserving of a place on your to-read piles!

I appreciate the thoughts and insights, some while we hiked up a mountain as I recall (!), of biochemist friend Dr. Janet Lindsley from the University of Utah. Likewise, Spiritopia spirit chemist and friend Chris Beatty, my one-time publisher, provided important guidance. Thanks to Kathy Brewer and Bronwyn Moore, who as environmental engineers have serious chemistry bona fides, but most important here are outstanding readers, reviewers, and editors (Kathy, to my great benefit, has helped me on multiple books). Thanks to Bill Gibson for his review and unique interpretation of story—while not a chemist, Bill can surely be considered an *al*chemist for his ability to turn book reviewing into a humorous endeavor!

I thank colleagues (and friends!) Lori Byron, MD, and Dr. Miranda Margetts, Professor at Montana State University. Both provided helpful comments on, and review of, BAT CAVE as it was nearing completion. And separately, both have played a special role in helping Montanans face the physical and mental health threats resulting from climate change.

Thanks to Dr. Marty Zaluski, friend, sometimes work colleague (and boss!), and Montana's State Veterinarian, for his special insights into critter disease. And thanks to Dr. Pete Coppolillo of Working Dogs for Conservation, for early-on, thoughtful discussions on the methods, capabilities, and limitations of using dogs to detect disease.

Thanks to Dr. Lois Alexander of the College of Southern Nevada, for her expert review of a near-final version of BAT CAVE, including her gentle guidance on techniques biologists employ in the field, including the use of electronic tags.

Book 1 in THE CRITTER CHRONICLES series, FISH TANK: A FABLE FOR OUR TIMES, has been used to inspire thought on climate change in classes from grade school through university. I am hopeful that BAT CAVE finds similar acceptance—here focused on disease, immigration, and more—and hence I am greatly honored and indebted to past and present education professionals who reviewed the book. Their insights on BAT CAVE's applicability to academic settings helped shape the book's final narrative. Thanks to Jody Ouradnik, Nancy Jordheim, Brent and Reese Jordheim, Joan Exley, and Kelsey Green for the time and effort they made to help me improve BAT CAVE as a tool of education, and as, I hope, a good read for all. And thanks to my last reviewer, sister Susie Iverson, for her unique copy editing abilities, even finding errors at the 11th hour before release!

As always, my thanks to Kate, my ever and always inspiration.

Also, thanks to you, dear reader, for spending some of your valuable time reading BAT CAVE: A FABLE OF EPIDEMIC PROPORTIONS. I so hope that you found the story challenging, perhaps disturbing yes, but also fun and enlightening. I hope the story has given you pause to think more broadly about the issues of our day, be they environmental or societal, and possibly spur you to action. And finally, thank you for supporting independent writers and publishers. For those of us with heaps of passion to write but short of marketing funds (or, admittedly, interest in self promotion) your help getting out the word is super important. Ratings are critical, and your five star review on Amazon, GoodReads, Google, Kobo, and similar really matter in this world. Thank you!

Author Bio

IN 2018, SCOTT Bischke served as the proposal coordinator and editor for a major grant focused on bats and disease. The work of the grant, which includes 24 researchers from 14 institutions around the world, is led by Dr. Raina Plowright, then at Montana State University, now at Cornell University.

Scott also served as Science Writer for the MONTANA CLIMATE ASSESSMENT (2017; see *montanaclimate.org*) and, subsequently, in the same role for the CLIMATE CHANGE AND HUMAN HEALTH IN MONTANA report in 2020, and the GREATER YELLOWSTONE CLIMATE ASSESSMENT in 2021. Scott served as an appointed member of Montana Governor Steve Bullock's Climate Solutions Council, and as such helped create the MONTANA CLIMATE SOLUTIONS PLAN (2020). He helped develop the city of Bozeman Municipal Climate Action Plan (task force co-chair, 2008) and Bozeman Community Climate Action Plan (task force member, 2011).

Along with these efforts, Scott's professional life has touched broadly on issues of resource management and climate change. He worked as a chemical engineering researcher at three national laboratories, as an environmental engineer for Hewlett-Packard, as the lab director for the Yellowstone Ecological Research Center, and currently as a science writer and facilitator specializing in Greater Yellowstone Area science and technology issues. Among those efforts, Scott served as facilitator for the Interagency Bison Management Plan Partners (federal, tribal, and state entities) for 14 years.

Scott lives with his spouse and best friend, Katie Gibson, in Bozeman, Montana. The couple has hiked, biked, and canoed in places far and wide. A common thread in all of Scott and Katie's travels has been their desire to immerse themselves in the peace, solitude, and tranquility of the natural world. The couple seeks out people, places, and activities that reinforce their desire to live a life filled with positive energy. Perhaps more simply, they seek to live a life that reflects their gratitude for being alive each and every day.

Scott has published numerous books before BAT CAVE, including:

- TRUMPELSTILTSKIN — A FAIRY TALE (MountainWorks Press 2016);
- FISH TANK — A FABLE FOR OUR TIMES, Book 1 in THE CRITTER CHRONICLES series (MountainWorks Press 2012);

- GOOD CAMEL, GOOD LIFE — FINDING ENLIGHTENMENT ONE DROP OF SWEAT AT A TIME (MountainWorks Press 2010);

- CROSSING DIVIDES — A COUPLES' STORY OF CANCER, HOPE, AND HIKING MONTANA'S CONTINENTAL DIVIDE (American Cancer Society 2002); and

- TWO WHEELS AROUND NEW ZEALAND — A BICYCLE JOURNEY ON FRIENDLY ROADS (Pruett Publishing hardback 1992; Ecopress 1996).

Scott's books are available in paperback, or in ebook format through Kindle, Google Books, or Kobo. A discussion guide for classrooms or book clubs is available for books in The Critter Chronicle series. You can find those guides, or contact Scott, via www.scottbischke.com. Or connect with him on Amazon, Goodreads, or Linked In.

Artist Bio

COLORADO-BASED ARTIST Katie Lindberg has been honing her drawing and painting skills for a lifetime. Katie explores a variety of media, but largely focuses on painting. She works across multiple scales, with efforts ranging from greeting cards to commissioned art to murals, including a major mural for the Denver Public school system. Since graduating from the University of Colorado Boulder (Go Buffs!), Katie has worked as an environmental engineer, an education and work life that have taught her to pay attention to detail while using her creativity to find solutions and bring ideas to life. Katie is also a budding entrepreneur and sometimes model.

Made in the USA
Monee, IL
21 October 2024